Magical
Awakening

By: Jessica Capasso

Dedication:

To my late father, Gene Wade, whose unbridled imagination and unique way of seeing things has shaped my world since my earliest years. Thank you Dad, for everything. Gene Wade 7/7/1955-7/8/2017 RIP

CONTENTS

Tiana By JRT

Tiana By JRT

ACKNOWLEDGMENTS

First of all, I would like to thank my dear friend Raine,
whose assistance in proofreading and offering open
feedback during the entire process was invaluable, as was
her beautiful illustrations that brought my characters to
life.
I would also like to thank my daughter, Anastasia who
designed the cover of this book with her incredible talent
and vision.
My late father and my mother, Gene and Barbara, offered
invaluable support to my writing endeavors through my
entire life and deserve the greatest thanks for putting up
with my eccentricities.
I also offer my thanks to all writers and creators that have
gone before for all their works that gave me inspiration
and ideas.

Staryn By JRT

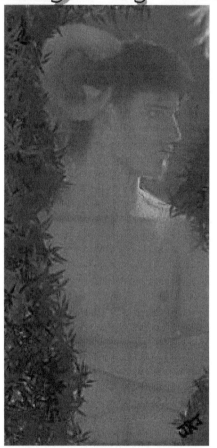

Prologue

Villagers the breadth of the continent hunkered in their homes as the storm season seemed to have come early. The ground quaked beneath them as the thunder rolled above. Roaring winds blew through the streets, taking anything that hadn't yet been secured along with them as lightning struck the ground with resounding cracks. There was a family though, that paid no attention to the storms raging around them, as they awaited their new arrival.

Frigen paced the floor as he listened to his wife's screams from the next room. The midwife had arrived just before the storms started, not long after Caria had gone into labor. It had been a difficult pregnancy and the midwife wasn't hopeful about the prognosis of the mother or the baby, which caused Frigen much distress. This was a late pregnancy for them. They were rapidly approaching old age, and had long thought Caria barren. It seemed like forever before Frigen finally heard the cry of a baby, though he could barely hear it over the roll of thunder and crack of lightning that came at the same time. As he rushed into the room to hold his new child, he didn't even notice the end of the storm.

He rushed into the room, just in time for his daughter to be thrust into his arms by the frantic midwife. Frigen didn't know much about birthing, but he knew, even without the midwife's frantic bustling, that the amount of blood between his wife's legs was not normal. Caria reached out her arms for the baby, and Frigen, with tears in his eyes, laid her on his wife's breast. "Tiana," she said weakly in awe as the pudgy little arm reached up for her, showing a white starburst birthmark on the inside of her right arm. No sooner than Frigen had noticed it, his attention was drawn back to his wife as she breathed her last and the newly christened Tiana began to cry once more, followed soon by her father, as the midwife slipped silently out of the room so as not to interrupt the family's mourning.

It was nearly an hour later and Frigen had not yet left his wife's side, when a young woman came in, carrying her own child of nearly six months. Frigen had been expecting her. She would nurse little Tiana until she was old enough to wean. He handed over the baby without a word, and Marla took her in her free arm and went to the sitting room to feed the newborn. They would discuss the details of the arrangement later. Frigen had not wanted to do so before, not wanting to

4

consider the possibility of his beloved wife not surviving the birth.

Marla stayed there, with both infants, until nightfall when Frigen finally exited his room. "You can take her with you until she is grown enough to not need you," he said wearily. He knew that it wasn't his daughter's fault that her mother died, but didn't think he could deal with her right now, and since she would need to be around Marla most of the time anyway, it would give him time to grieve in peace before he had to face her.

Marla simply nodded and took the bag he gave her with the things for Tiana. He would share his food and wares with her as long as Tiana was with her as well, as was customary in these arrangements. There was nothing odd about the infant residing with the wet nurse for the first year, especially when the mother didn't survive the birth and she had a husband and children at home already.

The villagers were nervous by the eerie stillness after the great storm. Generally, when Linaria's storm season began it didn't end for weeks, building slowly and then tapered off just as slowly. The sudden intensity and then the end was odd, and they didn't much like oddities. None of them connected the occurrence with the birth of Tiana though. None save her father and the midwife, who were the only ones who knew just how close the timing really was. The midwife did not speak of it, but avoided the child like the plague, leaving her medical care to her assistant.

Frigen also didn't speak of it for fear of losing his last link to his beloved wife and soon put it out of his mind altogether.

Tiana was a week old before Frigen felt up to facing her and was a frequent visitor to Marla's home after that. Marla and her family were delighted with the lovable child, and credited the rash of good luck that befell her family to the good karma generated by Marla's kindness in caring for her. Their crops were flourishing, they made it through the storm season with no damage to their home or belongings, her husband's hunts were always fruitful, and her children and Tiana were in perfect health. Frigen also had a similar string of good luck.

The real storm season on Linaria began when Tiana was only two weeks old, running the usual course, except that the storms weren't quite as strong at their peak as they usually were. The villagers credited that to the early storm, choosing to believe that it had gotten the worst of it out of the way beforehand. It was the only explanation they could come up with.

The entire village had a bountiful harvest that year, though Frigen's and Marla's put them all to shame. Frigen was even able to purchase a pair of goats that fall, which would give them fresh milk and cheese by the time Tiana came home. By the time the fall storm season rolled around, the villagers had more than enough food stored to get them through the winter, without any of the lean times that generally came later in the year.

By the time Tiana came home just before her first birthday, a few weeks in advance of the spring storm season, Frigen was completely enamored with her. He took her out to the porch every morning to watch Linaria's twin suns rise as he told her stories of her mother, who she was coming to resemble greatly as her light brown hair was growing to form delicate ringlets and her eyes darkened to the same nearly purple color as her mother's.

Frigen doted on his daughter. It wasn't until just after her second birthday that the strange storm at her birth was brought back to his mind when he noticed the strange occurrences that surrounded her. No matter how high the shelf was where he put things, she somehow always got her hands on what she wanted the instant his back was turned. He was able to ignore it for a while; when she would turn her innocent charming smile on him and he would melt.

It wasn't until he entered her room one day to find all of her toys dancing in the air around her that he couldn't ignore it anymore. He rushed in, swatting them out of the air before he picked her up in his arms and held her tightly, so tightly she cried out in pain, prompting him to loosen his grip slightly. "It's okay, papa. I only playing," she said sweetly, sensing his distress.

"Don't...Don't play like that Tiana. Please. Don't ever do that. Especially where anyone else can see," he said fearfully. He was brought back to his early fear of losing her should people find out what she was capable

7

of.

She bit her lip as it started to quiver. "I bad?" she asked worriedly.

"No baby. No, you're not bad. You just can't do stuff like that anymore. You understand?" he said nervously.

"Kay papa. I pwomise," she said solemnly.

Tiana did her best to keep her promise after that. There were times that she couldn't help herself and used her abilities to retrieve something she wanted, but her father never let himself notice. As long as she was subtle, he could pretend it wasn't happening. It was their little secret. One that he knew would end them both if it was ever learned. The strange providence that had befallen the village since her birth took a more sinister turn for him. He just couldn't see things the same way. He now knew, without question, that it had to do with her very presence and he became more than a little paranoid that other people would realize that too. He ended up keeping them locked away in their house more often than not, only venturing out into the village once a month for supplies.

The villagers talked about them often, thinking that the old man was losing his mind in grief for his wife. They had all noticed just how much Tiana looked like her mother, assuming that was what triggered it so late. They tried to coax him out more, but that just made him more paranoid, and when they tried to get Tiana to come out and play with the other children, his reaction quickly sent them on their way and increased the muttering about them. He never realized that his behavior was drawing far more attention than Tiana's presence ever could.

Tiana had just turned four years old when disaster struck and Frigen's secret was exposed. They had been visiting the village to stock up on supplies just as the storm season started, before they got too bad to travel. During this visit, a strong gust of wind blew the heavy sign off the apothecary's shop and it was headed right towards Frigen. Tiana threw out her hand instinctively to protect her father and the sign was deflected. Unfortunately, it was deflected right towards a young mother rushing into a storefront to get out of the weather. She and her baby were killed instantly, and the villagers were frozen in shock and fear, looking at Tiana as if she were evil.

Frigen, knowing that when they snapped out of it, things would go haywire, grabbed his daughter and ran with her, heading back home as quickly as he could. He started throwing everything he could find in bags, ready to leave his whole life behind and find a new place to live. Before he could leave though, he heard banging on the front door and he knew that he was out of time. He peeked through the curtains to see nearly the entire village gathered there.

"Worry not, Frigen. We have no quarrel with you. Send out the witch and we will leave you in peace," the magistrate told him calmly.

Frigen knew that there was no chance of them getting out of here now. He knew that they wouldn't stop until they got her. If it hadn't been for the death of the woman and baby he may be able to talk their way out of this, but that had to be answered for, and they would only accept one outcome. Tiana's execution for witchcraft and murder. He had apparently taken too long to think because the magistrate spoke again. "Send her out Frigen or we're coming in," he said warningly.

Frigen acted quickly. He took the bag of food and supplies and wrapped the straps firmly around Tiana's shoulders and whispered softly, "Go out the back and run. Go into the forest and keep running. Don't come back, no matter what."

"But papa. I can't leave without you," she said sniffling.

"You have to, baby. Don't worry. Use whatever you can to survive. Use your abilities. You'll be okay. Just go. Quickly," he said kissing her on the brow and giving her a push towards the door before saying louder, just loud enough for those outside to hear him, "Go to your room and lock the door Tiana. Papa will take care of this." Hopefully he could buy her enough time to get away.

Once the back door was closed behind her and he could make out her shape getting smaller as she approached the forest, he opened the front door and slipped out, not letting anyone in as he tried to talk the villagers down. He knew it was futile, but they were a generally peaceful people. They wouldn't be quick to harm an old man in their eagerness to get at Tiana. As long as they thought she was still in the house, they would be content to try and talk him down. At least for a little while.

When they gave up on talking and tried to push past him to get into the house, he pushed back, trying to buy every second he could for his precious girl to get as far away as possible. The crowd was quickly getting worked up into an angry mob and he knew it was all over when he punched the magistrate. Shortly after that, the people poured into the house leaving his broken and bloody body barely breathing on the stoop. He managed to drag himself over the threshold as he heard the crack of the doorframe to Tiana's room when they busted in. He heard a few more crashes and then they came out and started tearing the rest of the house apart as the magistrate came over to Frigen. "Where is she, old man?" he asked heatedly.

"Gone. You'll...never...get her," he breathed out in his last breath. The magistrate gave the body one more kick in anger before he joined the villagers in tearing the house down to its studs to make sure there were no hiding places possible before they headed towards the forest to search. How hard could it be to find a frightened child? Even if she did have an hour head start.

Chapter 1: Jaren

Jaren wheezed as he made his way back inside from tending his small garden. He had only managed to work out there for little more than an hour before he was too weak to continue. He knew that he was running out of time. He would have to send a missive to his son. The trader would come by next month, and he would make sure it was ready by then. It was time for the next generation to take over the vigil. He only hoped he could make it until his son arrived. He had waited too long. He knew that. He had so hoped he would live to see the arrival of the chosen one, though. He hoped it would be he who was able to start her on her path, but It seemed that it wasn't to be.

He made his way back inside and pulled out the ancient text, just to read it one last time. His eyesight was failing, making it difficult to read, but he was still able to manage, even if it was mostly by memory. His family had been living in this cabin in the middle of the forest for nearly a thousand years, not that much of the cabin was still as it had been back then. Almost all of it had been replaced due to needed repairs over the centuries. This was where they were tasked to wait, though. One day, magic would return to the world and the chosen bearer would be led here. He had the gifts ready, taking them out regularly to gaze at them, wondering what they were and what type of person would come for them.

Jaren had begun his vigil twenty years ago, at the death of his father, just after his eldest son had married. He had not spoken to another person other than the trader who happened by twice a year since then. This clearing was so deep in the forest that most dared not venture this far. There were many stories about this forest, and while most thought them flights of fancy, they did not dare test them. Only Jaren knew that they were true. That once upon a time, when magic filled the world, this forest was alive. Often in the past few years he had gotten the sense that they were waking, or were perhaps simply still pretending to sleep. He had hoped that it was a sign that the time was near, but perhaps it was simply a sign of senility.

It wasn't even twilight yet when Jaren found himself dozing in his chair, but he pulled himself to standing, with great effort, and gingerly placed the ancient book back in its drawer before dragging his weary body to his bed, quickly drifting off to sleep.

Tiana wasn't sure how long she had been running. Her legs had long since begun to ache, and her tears were dried on her cheeks. She ran until the sun had set and night fell over the forest. She broke off a chunk of bread to eat, and drank from a nearby stream before curling up in a bed of wet leaves and the tears flowed freely again as she cried herself to sleep as the storm raged around her. She was asleep before she saw the tree branches shifting overhead, shielding her from the worst of the rain. She was sleeping too deeply to notice the deer that curled around her to keep her warm.

When she woke the next morning, everything was as it had been when she had laid down. The tree branches were back to their normal place and the deer was already gone. Tiana was cold and frightened and hungry. She ate some more bread and drank from the stream again, not knowledgeable enough to know that the water shouldn't pool in her hands nearly as easily as it was and not seeing how clear it turned as she removed it from the murky stream. Such things were far beyond her notice right now. All she could think of was her father and how alone she was and hoping that he was alright and that he would find her. He told her to run though. To not turn back, and she had to listen to him, so when her belly was full, and her thirst was quenched, she picked up the now half empty bag and began to run again, putting more and more distance between her and the village that she had always called home.

She continued in this vein for four days. She ran out of food on the second day, but she stayed near the stream, so she still had access to water. The storms were picking up, so much so that had the forest not been protecting her, she likely wouldn't have survived. She failed to notice the movement of the trees to intercept any debris that the wind kicked up, or the way the roots sticking out of the ground moved out of her path as she ran. The forest knew that she wasn't in enough control of her powers yet to protect herself, so they would do it for her. She was their child. Their chosen. They kept her safe even as they herded her towards the sage.

Night had just begun to fall on the fourth day when she stumbled into a small clearing with a small unkempt garden. It was her devastating hunger that led her into it as she began to pull vegetables from the ground and eat them raw. Another heavy gust of wind rattled the old house and made her jump. She bit her lip nervously as she looked at the door. She couldn't remember what it was like to be dry. Or warm. She couldn't resist going inside just for a bit. All the lights were out so if anyone was there they must be asleep. She could sneak in, dry off, maybe sleep for a bit and then leave before anyone woke up. Maybe she could even get some more food for her journey.

She crept nervously up to the door and slipped inside as quietly as she could. The fire gave enough light for her to see, though the placement of it and the guard in front made the light very dim, but it had been darker outside. She made her way over to the wash basin and stripped out of her clothes, wringing them out over the basin as well as she could before replacing them. She made her way to the fire and stoked it like she had seen her father do, noticing that it was starting to die down and not wanting the occupants of the house to wake when it did. She bit her lip hard enough to draw blood in her efforts not to cry out when she burnt her hand, but she found that soaking it in the water in the wash basin helped to ease the sting. She had staved off the worst of her hunger in the garden, so her exhaustion took most of her mind and she made her way back to the plush bearskin rug in front of the fireplace and closed her eyes, only intending to sleep for a while.

Jaren woke slowly the next morning and drug himself out of bed, holding onto the wall for purchase as he made his way towards the kitchen to find some breakfast, only to stop short as he saw a small dirty child curled up on the rug in front of the fire. His first thought was that the chosen had come, but he quickly put that out of his mind. The chosen couldn't be starting the journey so young. It was just some lost child who wandered in out of the storm. The parents would likely be soon behind searching for her. He took his cane, knowing that he would need it to get back up again, and made his way over to her, kneeling next to her as he reached out to shake her shoulder gently. "Wake up, child. Are you hungry?" he asked gently.

Tiana startled awake and scrambled away from him fearfully. She knew she was in trouble now. She had trespassed and stolen his food and as if that weren't bad enough, if he found out that she was a...what was it the villagers had called her? A witch...he would surely kill her for it. She pressed herself as tightly into the corner as she could manage, not willing to brave trying to pass him to get to the door as the terror started to overwhelm her. "It's alright, child. Old Jaren's not gonna hurt you," he said soothingly as he crawled towards her, hand outstretched only to snap it back as she whimpered, and a web of vines seemed to grow out of the ground to encase her in a protective cocoon. "The chosen," he whispered in awe.

Tiana's whimpers turned to terrified sobs. Now she had done it again. Now he would know what she was. She remembered the fear in the villager's eyes when she had saved her father on that street. She remembered the fear in her father's eyes when he first saw her using her powers. She remembered the fear in his eyes again as he sent her away. She had known in that moment that they were going to kill her, and her fear had given her the strength to keep running, but she was trapped now. This was the end. "I'm sorry, I'm sorry, I'm sorry," she sobbed brokenly, not even hearing the soft words spoken just outside her little save haven.

When Jaren realized that she wasn't hearing him, he sat back on the floor, knowing that he would regret that later, and he began to sing a lullaby that his mother had sang to him as a child and that he had sang to his own children. He wasn't sure how long he sat there singing, but it couldn't have been too long because his stomach wasn't rebelling for breakfast yet. It was long enough for his old bones to start to ache though. Finally, he heard the sobs start to taper off and soon a small hole appeared in the vines and he could see a tiny frightened face peering out at him. "There now, that wasn't so hard, was it? I promise I won't hurt you, little one. Why don't you come out of there and we can find something to eat hmm?"

Tiana was still scared, but some part of her

couldn't help but trust him. That didn't mean she would let him get too close. She was a fast runner when she needed to be. He did offer her food though and she was terribly hungry. The vines slowly drew away as she made the decision to come out and he smiled brightly at her. She skirted along the wall, staying out of arm's reach as he struggled to his feet. When she saw how much trouble he was having moving around she rushed into the kitchen ahead of him. "I can get the food for us," she offered, hoping to earn a little more by helping out.

Jaren considered it for a moment. On one hand, he didn't really want to put her to work, but she seemed eager to help and could definitely take care of it faster than he could. "Very well. The bread is in the cabinet there and the jam is under the counter next to the wash basin. There is milk from the goats out under the stoop," he told her. He had just milked the goats last night and it was still cool enough with the storms that it would be good for another day or two. He definitely wasn't going to put her to that much work getting fresh milk. He noticed how her face lit up at the mention of jam and milk and he wondered how long she had been wandering alone and where her parents were.

Tiana went out to get the milk first and for a moment she considered making a run for it, but her stomach had other ideas. She could still run later if she needed to. He was old and slow. He wouldn't be able to catch her. As long as she was careful, and especially didn't let him get between her and the door, she could make it through this and even get a nice meal. The final decision was made when a bolt of lightning and a loud boom of thunder shook the cottage. She didn't want to go back out there now. She scrambled back into the house with the milk and set it on the table and went for the bread, jam, and plates and cups which Jaren directed her to.

It wasn't until Tiana set the plate in front of him that he noticed the blistered burn on her hand, and he just managed to stop himself before he grabbed her arm to get a better look at it. She was still so skittish that it would probably send her running again and he didn't have the strength to chase her. Instead, he spoke softly, "What happened to your hand?" Tiana quickly hid it behind her back guiltily and looked away. "It's alright, child. You can tell me," he prodded gently.

"I...the...your fire...it was going down...I wanted to fix it...I did fix it...I just..."

"Oh, you poor child. You shouldn't have had to do that. I was just so tired last night, I forgot to stoke it before I went to bed. I'm sorry, little one," he said sadly.

Tiana looked at him with wide eyes. He was apologizing to her? She had snuck into his house in the night, played with fire like she knew she wasn't supposed to, and he was apologizing to her for it? It didn't make sense and she wanted to make sure he knew that she didn't deserve it, so she confessed what else she had done last night. "I...I also...I ate some of your food...in the garden. I'm sorry. I was just so hungry," she sniffled as she backed slowly towards the door, ready to make a run for it.

"It's quite alright, little one. I don't think I would have had the strength to harvest it anyway. It couldn't have been very good though. I know that none of it was quite ready and it wasn't even cooked. You really must have been hungry." She nodded through her tears. "I am not angry, child. Truly. I am only glad that you were able to get something to eat, poor though it may have been. Please. Sit. Eat."

She sat gingerly at the table and he motioned her towards the plate that he had filled with sliced bread and jam while they had been talking and she watched him warily as she picked it up and began to eat. When he just smiled warmly at her and picked up his own bread to begin eating, she dug in with gusto, filling her mouth almost faster than she could chew. Jaren chuckled and said, "Slow down, little one. I won't take it away before you're finished."

She mumbled something that he couldn't understand with all the food in her mouth and he tilted his head questioningly at her. She chewed quickly and swallowed what was in her mouth and then tried again. "Tiana. My name is Tiana," she said before she began eating quickly again.

"That's a beautiful name, Tiana. Maybe after breakfast you'll let me put some poultice on your burn and wrap it up?" he asked hopefully.

She could feel the fear welling up in her again at the thought of letting him get that close and even touch her, but he was being so kind to her. He was giving her food and he seemed to forgive her for what she'd done. She couldn't even see the fear in his eyes that she had seen in the others who wanted to hurt her, so she nodded nervously.

Jaren considered telling her about herself, but decided that it could wait. According to the prophecies she would be here until the end of the storm season for three more weeks. He would have time. It would be better if he could earn her trust a little bit first. He also wanted to know what had happened to her. How she had come to be so far from civilization all alone and hungry enough to eat raw un-ripened vegetables straight from the ground. He knew that it was too soon for that story too though. He had to make her feel safe first. Safe enough to talk. Safe enough to stay. This was the moment he had been waiting his entire life for. He wasn't going to risk ruining it by being impatient.

They finished their breakfast in silence, and she hadn't taken her eyes off him the entire time. She seemed both curious and wary of him all at once. Once they were finished eating, she took the plates and cups over to the wash basin and rinsed them off, jumping away when she heard his chair move as he struggled to get up. "It's okay, Tiana. I'm just going to get the poultice and bandages for your hand," he tried to reassure her.

"I can get them," she said quickly. She could tell that it hurt him to move around, plus she wanted him to stay where she could see him and knew where he was.

"They are too high for you to reach," he told her. "In that cabinet up there," he pointed up above the counter. She hesitated for a moment before she decided that he had already seen her use her powers and didn't seem to mind so she just reached out her good hand and the needed items flew out of the cupboard into it as she watched carefully for his reaction. "Handy, that," he said with a chuckle. "Come. Sit. Let us get that hand of yours fixed up."

She sat in the chair next to him, between him and the door, and reached out her burned hand nervously. He took it with great care, very gently spreading the poultice over the burn, apologizing when she whimpered in pain, before wrapping the bandage around it. "There now. All done. Doesn't that feel better?"

She tested moving her hand and found that the poultice had numbed the pain. "Thank you," she said softly moving back away from him again. "I should go," she said tentatively looking towards the door.

"Nonsense. You should stay until the storms stop. I don't want you going out there and getting hurt or sick," he told her.

She considered it for a moment. It was a kind offer and he seemed nice enough. She didn't really want to go back out into the storm anyway, but her father had told her to keep running. Maybe she had run far enough for now. Maybe she could take a break. Maybe he really wouldn't hurt her. She would still be careful though. "Okay. Til the storms stop," she agreed.

Jaren nodded. He wished he could offer her a place for longer. He wished he wouldn't have to send her away at all, but the prophecies were clear. She could only stay until the storms ended. "I'm afraid I have little to do here to occupy little girls," he admitted apologetically.

She just shrugged and went to finish cleaning their breakfast dishes before started straightening the house. She had often helped her father with the housework, so she knew what to do. When Jaren protested that she didn't need to do that, she just told him it was better than being bored. In reality, she was overawed by his kindness and wanted to do something to deserve it.

Jaren wasn't much of a slob and generally kept things cleaned up so there wasn't much to do, and the house was as clean as she could get it within an hour. Jaren decided he could start warming her up to the idea of magic at least, so he started telling her stories. Stories of days gone by, back when magic lit the world. He amused her with tales of magical creatures and humans who could use magic. Some of it had come from stories passed down from his family, some of it he made up, and some of it came from the ancient text he still had. There was very little written down though. It was mostly just the prophecies, but he had figured out a few things from there.

When the suns began to set, Jaren considered the sleeping arrangements. He wanted to offer her his bed, but he knew that he would never manage to sleep on the floor or get up the next morning if he did, and he doubted she would consent to sharing his bed, even if it weren't completely improper to do so. In the end, he decided that she had seemed comfortable enough on the bearskin rug, and it was rather plush. He would get her a pillow and blanket though at least.

For the first time in what felt like forever to the four-year-old girl, Tiana had three meals that day, was warm and dry, and fell asleep curled up by a fire. The tears still flowed as she lay there waiting for sleep to take her though. She missed her father. She missed her home. And she had no idea what was coming next.

Chapter 2: Wishing

Despite Jaren's kindness, Tiana still didn't feel safe here. She wasn't sure if she would ever feel safe again really. So, when Jaren shook her awake the next morning for breakfast, she once again scrambled into the corner before she remembered where she was. Jaren held his hands out welcomingly. "It's alright, little one. You're safe here," he assured her. She didn't want to argue with him, so she just nodded and headed to the kitchen to grab the bread and jam and went out to grab the milk while Jaren sliced the bread and spread the jam. She noticed that they would probably finish the milk this morning, and started making plans to get some more.

She got her chance around midday, shortly after they finished lunch, when Jaren dozed off in his chair. She slipped outside with the milk pail, braving the storm, and headed to where she had noticed the goat. She had never helped her father with this particular chore, but she had watched him often enough, and it hadn't looked very hard. She got nervous for a minute when the goat seemed ready to rebel against her, but she just put a hand on her neck and talked softly to her for a moment and she calmed quickly. She wasn't sure why her hand was tingling where it touched her, but didn't worry about it at all.

Tiana was small enough that she didn't even need

a stool as she took the goats teats and started to pull like she'd seen her father do, but nothing happened. She tried a few more times before she stamped her foot in frustration and tried one last time. Once again, her hand tingled as the milk finally started flowing. When the small bucket was full, she carried it inside as quietly as she could. She would put it in the jars later, and she headed back out to try and do something with the garden. If Jaren was going to keep feeding her, then she should pull her weight. She could tell he couldn't really do much with it anymore and wondered what he would do when she was gone. For the first time, she let herself consider staying here long term. Surely the villagers weren't still looking for her and maybe if she stayed put, her father might find her.

She puttered around the garden for a while, pulling weeds and setting things to rights. She wasn't sure how long she was out there, but after a while she heard the cottage door open and Jaren called, "Tiana?" so she ran back to the house and he stepped aside to let her in. "Oh, you silly child," he gently admonished. "What were you doing out there in the storm?"

"I was taking care of the garden," she said proudly. "And I got some more milk from the goats."

Jaren just chuckled at her exuberance as he handed her a towel to dry off. "You didn't need to do that," he told her. "I was going to go do that this afternoon."

"That's okay. I like helping. I used to help Papa all the time in the gardens. The goats were hard though," she admitted.

"I can't believe they didn't hurt you," he said looking her over as if to make sure she really was unharmed. "They usually get rather perturbed at the process." Tiana just shrugged and once she was as dry as she was going to get, she went over to start pouring the milk in the jars. As he watched her he started to get an idea. "I wonder…" he said thoughtfully, and she looked curiously at him. Once the bucket was empty, he dipped it in the wash basin and filled it about halfway with water. "Can you make this water freeze?"

"How?" she asked confused.

"How did you bring the stuff from the cabinet yesterday?" he asked in response.

"I don't know. I just…kinda…wished it, I guess."

"Then just wish the water to freeze," he told her with an encouraging smile.

"I don't know if I can," she said sadly, not wanting to let him down.

"It's okay if you can't. I just want to see if you can," he prodded gently. If he could get her using her powers more consciously maybe it would be easier for her to accept what he would have to tell her soon.

"I'll try," she said as she reached a hand for the bucket. She concentrated on what it felt like when she called the stuff from the cabinet and the water splashed out at her. Jaren chuckled lightly and motioned for her to try again. She thought that maybe she was trying to call the water to her, so she just focused on the wishing feeling and thought of the water being ice. It worked. A little too well. The water in the pail was now solid ice, as was the water left in the wash basin, and the water that was left on her, leaving her clothes rather stiff and she huffed in annoyance as Jaren laughed cheerfully. She had noticed that same tingling feeling in her hand though, and finally realized what it might be. "I...um...I think I might have...done something like that with the goats," she said nervously, hoping he would take it as well as her other oddities.

"What? Turned them to ice?" he teased good-naturedly.

Tiana couldn't help the giggle that escaped. "No," she said as though it should be obvious. "I mean...like...used my wishing thing."

"That would make sense," Jaren said nodding. "That would explain why they were docile enough to let you get the milk."

"Docile?"

"Calm," he corrected.

"Maybe we shouldn't drink the milk," Tiana said nervously. She knew that it was supposed to be a bad thing. At least that's what her father thought, and the villagers.

"Nonsense. It wouldn't have hurt it any. If anything, it might have helped it," he told her. "That wishing thing you do. It's called magic."

"Magic? Like in your stories?" She asked wide-eyed.

"That's right," he told her. He wasn't going to go into the prophecies yet, but he could tell her that much.

"How come I can do it but no one else can? Everyone thinks it's bad," she said sadly.

"You can do it because you're special, and it's not bad. It just tends to scare people because they can't do it and that's why they don't like it," Jaren told her.

"But I…" Tiana started and then stopped herself before she said anything else. She didn't want him to know what she had done. He would surely send her away then, if not hurt her himself.

"You what, little one?" he asked gently seeing that something had scared her.

"Nothing," she said quickly, and he could see she wasn't going to budge so he let it drop for the time being. Maybe she would feel safe enough to open up to him eventually. In the meantime, all he could do was try to build trust. He wasn't really qualified to teach her about her powers. That was a job for someone else. But he could at least show her that she had them and could use them consciously. He could see that she was uncomfortable with the idea now, so he let it drop. It was getting close to dinnertime, so he let her help him make dinner, mostly in silence.

While they were working Tiana was lost in thought. Now that she had time to think and was relatively comfortable, she couldn't stop thinking about the lady and her baby that had died. That she had killed. She knew that was unforgivable. She was questioning her father's order for her to run. He had always said that when she did something bad she should just accept the punishment. Why had he made her run away from it?

Maybe he thought being out there alone and hungry in the storm was a better punishment than what the others had in mind. But she wasn't out there. She was warm and comfortable, with enough food, and sheltered from the storm. Jaren was so nice to her though, and he really didn't want her to go. He acted like her leaving would be punishing him and he didn't deserve to be punished. He hadn't done anything wrong.

She kept up her silence through dinner and then went to lay down on her makeshift bed, still lost in thought and guilt. Nightmares kept her up most of the night that night, but she had thankfully not been loud enough to wake Jaren. Her dreams had been filled with the faces of the woman and baby, the woman yelling at her, and the faces of the villagers. In the nightmares they caught her and killed her and that's usually when she woke up crying. For the first time, she was awake before Jaren and when she heard him getting up, she already had breakfast on the table. After breakfast, she asked softly, "Can I go work in the garden for a little while?"

Jaren considered the idea for a moment. It wasn't good for a child to be cooped up inside all the time, especially when there was nothing to do, and the garden did need to be tended, storm or no storm. When the storms last more than a month at a time, it wasn't an uncommon thing. It still wasn't good for her to be out there for too long though. "Only until lunch," he told her. She nodded and ran out the door, not noticing his frown as she did. Whatever melancholy had struck her while they were talking yesterday, seemed to still have hold of her, and maybe it was his imagination, but she seemed tired. He felt very out of his depth. He didn't know how to cheer her up. His children had always talked to him when they were upset, but he didn't know how to get her to open up, and if he didn't know what was bothering her, he didn't know what to do about it.

He decided to turn his mind to seeing what he could figure out given the information she had given him. She had mentioned helping her father before, but she hadn't mentioned a mother. She had been terrified of being hurt by him, especially when she first showed her powers. She said that people were afraid of her, and seemed like she was about to offer some proof that her powers really were bad. Had something happened where she was from? Had there been an accident? She was obviously running from something, and he wondered if her father was part of the problem or if he had tried to protect her. She didn't speak of him with fear though, so maybe he helped her escape. He knew enough about the villagers to know that it wouldn't have boded well for him if he had. He remembered the line of the prophecy that said that she would come to him drowning in sorrow and death. It was his job to repair some of that damage and help her come to terms with it, but how to get her to talk. They still had more than two weeks together. He would give it a little more time before he started pushing. Prophecy had a way of offering its own solutions. Maybe something would happen that would prompt her to open up. In the meantime, he could at least try to cheer her up.

While she was working in the garden, he began to search the house for anything that could be used as a toy before he lit on an idea. He pulled out his stack of parchment and ink. He could let her draw. Children liked to draw, and he wouldn't need them much longer. He knew that he wouldn't have long after she left. He wondered if he had only lasted this long because it was his destiny to be here for her. He only hoped that it wouldn't be his death that would send her on the next part of her journey. That he could hold out until after she left. She didn't need to see that. While he had some time free, he pulled a piece of parchment to himself and dipped the quill in the ink. He still had a missive to write to his son. It would just be a little different than he had planned last week.

Arden,

The event we have all been waiting for has come to pass. The chosen has arrived, and our long vigil is over. She is so young though. Far too young, but there is naught we can do about that. You are free to live the remainder of your life as you see fit. I will not make it back to town when she leaves. I am reaching the end of my life and doubt that I would be able to make the journey. I wish you and your family well. I miss you my son.

Until we meet again,
Jaren

That done, he folded the parchment and sealed it, setting it at the corner of the counter for the trader to find in case he was gone when the young man arrived, and then set to starting a stew for lunch. When it was ready he called Tiana in and helped her to dry off. He had pulled out one of his old shirts and had her change into that since her dress was beyond dirty and rather ragged by this point. He would try to fix it after lunch. He didn't have any children's clothes and wasn't much good at sewing, but he could try and patch up the holes at least. His shirt went all the way down to her ankles, and since she didn't have any other clothing he had the idea to create a makeshift belt and give her some more of his shirts when he sent her on her way. It would at least be something she could change into.

He was glad to see that the time outside had done her some good. She wasn't nearly as sad as she had seemed before, though she still seemed just as tired. So much so that he talked her into taking a nap after lunch and even sent her to his bed for it while he sat in his chair and took the moment alone to re-read the ancient prophecies. He wanted to make sure that he hadn't forgotten anything this close to the end. He replaced the book in the drawer when he heard her starting to stir. He didn't want to have to answer any questions about it just yet. When she came out, still rubbing her eyes, he smiled softly at her. "I found some spare parchment and ink if you want to draw for a little while," he offered motioning to the desk and the smile that lit her face was contagious as she rushed over there.

"How much can I use?" she asked hopefully.

"As much as you want. I only put out what I could spare," he told her cheerfully. She didn't need to know that it was all he had. She didn't need to know that he was dying and wouldn't need any more. "Just remember that it has to last until you leave," he reminded her.

The grin on her face just got brighter as she looked wide-eyed at the stack. Her father let her draw sometimes, but he didn't want to waste too much parchment, so it wasn't often. She was used to conserving and drew small, using every available inch. She didn't even notice when Jaren started dinner, and when he called her to eat, she had barely made a dent in the stack. She would easily be able to make it last until the storms were over.

After they ate, Jaren asked, "Can I see your drawings? Maybe you could tell me about them?"

"Okay!" she said cheerfully and brought over what she had. She pointed out her father, and some of her favorite toys that she had left behind. When she could remember, she told him about how she got them and what she used to do with them. She had drawn the goats that they had and told him about them too. He noticed that she didn't talk much about her father, despite drawing him quite well, and wondered if that was too painful a subject for her right now. When they went to bed soon after, they were both in far better spirits than they had been the night before and Jaren was glad that he was able to cheer her up.

Tiana was glad that she didn't have any nightmares that night and she was woken for breakfast the next morning feeling well rested. They quickly worked out a routine. She would spend the morning working in the garden and milking the goats until lunch, and then the afternoons drawing. After dinner, she would tell Jaren all about her drawings. She let him do most of the cooking, but she did all the cleaning. She even got him to teach her how to wash her own clothes, but he wouldn't let her wash his. All in all, she was getting more and more comfortable here, and even felt almost safe as the storms began to taper off.

Chapter 3: Destiny

It was about a week before the storms were due to end when Jaren heard hoofs marching through the forest. It was too early for the trader to be there. He never came until after the storms ended. He wasn't sure who it was, but he didn't want to take any chances of it being one of the people who ran Tiana off from her home. She was sitting at the desk drawing and he said, "Tiana, someone's coming. Take all your drawings and go into the bedroom and be quiet."

She bit her lip fearfully and quickly did as she was told. As if the fear of who it might be wasn't bad enough, she was flashing back to when her father told her to run away, but then pretended to tell her to go to her room. Jaren took another quick look around the room to make sure that there was no sign that Tiana had been there before he opened the door.

It turned out that it was the trader after all. "You're early," Jaren said curiously.

"I was worried about you. I set out as soon as it was safe to travel. There's a witch running around these woods."

"A witch?" he asked feigning curiosity.

"Yes. She's already killed two people directly, one of them a baby, and bewitched an old man into sacrificing his life so she could escape," the trader told him.

Jaren forced himself not to react to that. He was starting to understand what had Tiana so scared now. He asked the questions he would be expected to ask. "Bewitched him how?"

"I don't know, but he held off the magistrate and started a fight that got him killed to give her time to escape and she headed into these woods."

"What does she look like?" he asked despite knowing the most probable answer to that question.

"When she was in the village she was posing as a little girl. Curly brown hair and purple eyes, according to the villagers. You should probably come back into town for a while to be safe."

"No. I'm fine here. I haven't seen any sign of her and I doubt I will. If she's on the run, she will avoid anyone in the area," Jaren told him and suddenly wanted to get rid of him, so he could go to Tiana. If she was listening, she was probably horribly upset by now.

"Alright. If you're sure. I'll unload your usual supplies. You got anything for me to take into town?"

Jaren handed over the letter he had written to his son, knowing that the traders next stop on his route after him was the town his son lived in. He watched as his supplies were put away. He wanted to tell him to just go, but that would draw suspicion. The trader had been putting his supplies away for him for the last two years, ever since he started having trouble getting around on his own. It seemed like forever before the hoofbeats were trailing away from the cottage and he rushed into the room to find Tiana pressed into the corner, knees pulled to her chest and sobbing silently. Jaren sat on the bed next to her and she flinched away from him, but didn't seem to care much about anything else. "Are you gonna punish me now?" she asked through her sobs.

"No, little one. I'm not," he said gently. He was very worried that she didn't even seem ready to fight the idea any more. She seemed ready to accept whatever fate he decided to bring down on her and that said a lot about her current state of mind, and none of it good. "Do you wanna tell me what happened?" he prodded gently.

"It...it was...an accident," she said brokenly. "T-the sign...it was falling...headed for Papa...I didn't...didn't want him to be hurt. I just...just wished it away from him. I didn't mean...I didn't want it to hit anyone else...I-I'm s-sorry."

Jaren could feel his own tears prickling his eyes as he thought of what it must have been like for her, to see that, and to know that she was the cause of it. He reached down and lifted her up, even more alarmed that she didn't even try to struggle. He set her next to him on the bed and wrapped an arm around her. "It's okay, little one. It was just an accident. It wasn't your fault," he said soothingly.

"P-papa. That man...he said...said papa's..." she couldn't finish the sentence, but Jaren knew what she meant and guessed correctly that he was the old man that tried to protect her.

"I'm so sorry, little one," he said sadly, still holding

her close as she sobbed. "But you must never forget that he wanted you to go on. He gave himself to give you a chance to live. Do not throw that away." She was far too young to understand this. She shouldn't have to be dealing with it, but he was afraid for her. He was watching her spark go out. She didn't care what happened to her anymore, and he hoped it was just the shock of it, but he had to make sure that she snapped out of it. The sooner, the better. They didn't have much time left. "Please, Tiana. Promise me that you'll keep going. Always."

"How?" she asked heartbroken. "I...I don't know...if I can."

"You must," he told her gently. He wasn't sure if now was the best time to tell her about the prophecies and her destiny, but he had to give her something to fight for. Something to work for. She had lost everything and without something to hold on to, she could be lost. "You have a big destiny, child. There is much for you to do still." She didn't respond, but her sobs were beginning to diminish and eventually they drifted to a stop and he could tell she was dozing off. He laid her down on the bed and covered her up. "Sleep, child. We will talk more later," he said softly, pressing a kiss to her brow.

Jaren shuffled out of the room and pulled out the ancient texts to study as he waited for her to wake up. It was time. He knew that she wouldn't sleep for long. She was just exhausted from the emotional outburst. He suspected it would be nightmares that woke her, but hoped for the best. Unfortunately, that wasn't to be. She was sniffling when she emerged from the bedroom an hour later, but she plastered a brave look on her face as she came over to sit in the chair next to him. "What did you mean?" she asked curiously.

Jaren had been considering where to begin, and had a plan all mapped out. He patted the book in his lap to draw attention to it as he said, "This is a book of ancient prophecies. Prophecies are something that someone saw long before they ever happened. They know the future. This was written about two thousand years ago. See, magic used to be a big part of the world. Everything was part of magic. Even people. The people who could use magic were called a lot of things…"

"Like witches," she said sadly.

"Yes, that is one of the names they went by. People now think of witches as a bad thing though, so I don't recommend using it. They also went by magicians, sorcerers, enchanters, and even gods. It's not clear what happened really, but there were a lot of wars and fighting between them, until magic finally died. The last two gods, as they then called themselves, killed each other right here in this clearing and my family was told to wait here…for you."

"Me?" she asked wide-eyed.

"Yes. The prophecies said that one day, magic would return and the one who could use it would be led here, so my family was asked to wait here for you. My father and his father and his father, all the way back for a thousand years."

"Does that mean I can stay with you?" she asked hopefully.

This was the part that Jaren dreaded. If he had ever dreamed that the chosen one would come to him so young he could have prepared himself, but he had always assumed that she would at least be a teenager, if not an adult by the time she started on her journey. "I'm so sorry, little one. I wish you could. I would do anything for you to be able to stay here, at least until you're older, but the prophecies are clear. You have to go when the storms stop. You have to continue your journey," he said sadly.

"But...why? I won't be any trouble. I promise. And I can help with stuff. Like I have been. I won't eat much..."

He had to cut her off. He couldn't hear any more. His heart was breaking for her. "It's not so simple, little one. If it were up to me I would let you stay forever, but if you stay, you will die, and evil will take over the world before eventually destroying it." Tiana bit her lip fighting against the tears threatening to flow. "Don't worry. You won't be alone for long," he assured her, wanting to give her at least some comfort. "You will find a guide to help you and travel with you."

"Why can't you be my guide?" she asked, voice trembling.

"That is not my role. I am 'the sage' according to prophecy. I have some things for you when you leave, to make your journey easier. Even if I could take on the role of your guide, I am too old. I can't move around like

41

I used to. I can't travel with you and I wouldn't know where you need to go. Your guide will. I know this is a big job for such a little girl, but you'll be alright. I promise. You just have to be brave and strong like I know you can be."

"I...I'll try," she said as the tears flowed, but she wiped them away and plastered a brave look on her face.

"Chin up, child. You can still stay here for a while yet. You will stay until the storms end," he told her. "And I will teach you everything I know, little as it is, before then." She nodded resolutely, and he smiled encouragingly at her. "But now, it is time to start on dinner," he said as he pulled himself to his feet.

She went over to wash the vegetables before he chopped them and asked, "So what else does it say about me in the book?"

"There is not much about you specifically. Most of it is about the death of magic and what the world would be like without it. You don't come in until the end. See the thing about prophecies is they don't always make a lot of sense, and they get harder to understand the farther in the future they are. What I've already told you, is easy enough to understand, but there is a lot that I don't understand, and can't understand without seeing it happen. For example, it said that you would arrive drowning in sorrow and death, but I didn't know what that meant until I met you and learned about your past."

"Oh," she said sadly, looking down and fighting

tears again at the reminder.

"You will take the book when you go though. I know you won't be able to read it yet, but perhaps your guide can. It will help you understand more as you go along."

"But it's yours," she protested.

"No, child. I have simply been holding it for you. It has always been meant for you, along with the other things I will give you," he told her.

"Like what?" she asked curiously.

"There is what looks like an egg of some sort, but I'm not sure what kind, and an old horn. See when you leave here, you will find danger soon. When you do, you have to blow the horn."

"And the horn will help?" she asked.

"Yes. But I don't know how. That is one of those things that I don't understand," he told her.

"What does it say?"

"It just says that the ancients of the forest will take you to their heart."

She scrunched up her nose as she thought about that. "I don't get it," she finally said.

"Neither do I, child. Neither do I," he said understandingly. The remainder of the cooking and the meal passed in silence and Jaren was feeling a little better about the situation. He could tell that she was still distraught, but he had given her something to think about. Something to live for, and that showed in her demeanor. He hated that she was being forced to grow up so fast though. He hated the burden that now rested

43

on her shoulders and vowed that he would help her to carry it as much as he could before she was forced to leave.

Tiana was still tired from all the emotions of the day, so she went to bed soon after dinner, but sleep was a long time coming. She kept thinking about the prophecies and what she had to do. She was afraid, but she remembered what Jaren said about her being brave and strong and she was determined not to let him down. When she finally did fall asleep, she slept soundly and didn't wake until Jaren woke her for breakfast and she had more questions for him. "You said the last two people like me died here, how?"

"I don't know the details, but I know that they were enemies. There was a big fight and they both killed each other at the same time. Did you see that old black oak tree out near the woodline?" he asked, and she nodded. "That's supposed to be where it happened. That tree sprung up at the spot that magic died."

"Why was it your family that had to wait here?"

"We had always served the god that lived here, but one of my ancestors was the one to betray him to his enemy and caused the final battle. To try to make up for it, my family was tasked to wait here for the chosen one who would come to return magic to the world," he explained.

"You got punished because of what someone else did?" she asked distastefully.

"No. It is not a punishment, but a duty. If he had lived, we would be serving him still. It's not so bad here.

It's nice to live out the end of one's life in peace and solitude after all. I got to live out in the world, married, had children, a good life. Then when my father got too old to continue, I came to take his place, as my son would have come to take my place soon had you not come when you did," he explained.

"You didn't mind having to wait here alone so long?" she asked confused. She couldn't imagine wanting to spend so much time alone.

"Not at all. You will find, when you reach my age, that it is tiring to deal with people all the time. Some peace and solitude is a precious thing," he told her with a smile. "But it is nice to have some company from time to time as well," he added, not wanting her to think that she was intruding and the smile she shot him told him that she understood.

The remainder of the week was spent with Jared teaching Tiana everything he knew and thought he had figured out about magic and teaching her how to read. He knew that he wouldn't be able to finish. They didn't have nearly enough time for her to learn completely, but he could get her started and make it easier for her later. She asked a lot of questions and he answered them as best he could. Then they day finally came. Jaren woke to the sun shining in the windows and knew it was time. He let out a weary sigh as he got out of bed.

Jaren stood there and watched her sleep for a few minutes, not wanting to disturb her just yet, before he went to the kitchen to get their breakfasts ready. He knew that he was pushing things, but didn't have the heart to send her out on an empty stomach. Only when it was ready, did he wake her. She noticed the sun shining too, and knew it was time for her to go, so it was a silent meal and the sadness was almost palpable in the room. When they were done eating, Tiana started to clean up as she normally did while Jaren went to get the bag that she had arrived with. In it, he placed two large loaves of bread, a jar filled with water, three of his shirts with the rope they had been using as a belt, and the book. There was no room for more in the bag, so he had to find something else for the egg.

By the time she was finished with the breakfast dishes, he had fashioned a sling for her to hold the egg in and taken out the horn as well. "It's time to go, Tiana," he said sadly.

"I can stay and take care of the garden and milk the goats for you again. I can still leave after lunch," she offered hopefully.

"I'm sorry, little one. I fear you have stayed too long already," he told her holding back his own tears.

She nodded sadly and ran to him and hugged him tightly. "I'll miss you," she said, sniffling.

"I'll miss you too, child."

"I'll never forget you," she vowed.

"Nor will I," he said giving her one more squeeze before she let go. He helped her get the sling around her neck and settle the egg against her stomach, draped the cord for the horn over it so that the horn rested just below the egg, and then got the bag over her shoulders. "Go on, little one. And good luck," he said with a watery smile.

"Goodbye," she said as the tears streaked down her cheeks, but she walked away anyway, stopping every so often to look back at him as he stood on the stoop watching her go. When she entered the forest in the direction he had pointed her, past the black twisted oak, he turned and went back inside and sat sadly in his chair. The place suddenly felt far more empty than it ever had before. He closed his eyes for a moment against the sadness, not realizing that they would never open again.

Chapter 4: Staryn

A young boy, barely a teenager respectively, sat at the base of a large tree, gazing up at it in rapt attention. "It is time, young Staryn. The chosen has begun her journey."

The boy looked horrified as he reached up to run a finger through his hair, stopping to scratch his horns that were just starting to come in. "It can't be. It's too soon. You said humans age slower than I do. She can't be more than a little sproutling still," he said in denial.

"She is too young. As are you. But it has begun regardless," the ancient tree told him.

"But I can go find her and bring her here. You can teach us both until we're older," he protested.

"No. It cannot be. What has begun must not be halted or it will be the ruin of us all," the tree said firmly.

"But I'm not ready yet. I still have so much to learn," Staryn said fearfully.

"You are ready. You must be. There is no more time," the tree said sadly. "You must go now, Staryn. Guide the chosen as you were born to do."

Staryn knew there was no more point in arguing and hung his head even as he got to his feet, leaning down to brush the leaves and dirt from the light brown fur that covered him from the waist down. "I will do my best," he said nervously.

"And that is all we can ask, child," the old tree said as one of the branches came forward to brush against the young satyr's face before it gave him a gently push towards the edge of the grove. Staryn looked back sadly as he passed out of sight and the old tree whispered sadly, "Be safe, my son."

Tiana hadn't thought it was possible to feel even more alone than she had when she had first set out from her home, but she did. She was just as scared too, but it was for a different reason this time. She wasn't afraid of the villagers coming after her. It was worse. She was terrified of the destiny that awaited her. Terrified that she wasn't good enough, or strong enough, or brave enough. Terrified that she would fail. She was no longer running away from something. She was now going toward something much more frightening and she wasn't in much of a rush to get there.

She walked at a decent pace through the forest, hoping she was still going the right way, but not really able to orient herself. She remembered what Jaren said about the forest leading her to him, and she hoped it was leading her still. It worried her that she was now walking away from the stream, but Jaren had told her that she should be able to use her powers to keep the water jar full and if not, that the forest would provide what she needed. His faith fed her own. He was so sure that she would be alright and taken care of that she couldn't help but believe it too.

"Was he right?" she asked the trees as she walked. "Will you really take care of me?" She wondered if she imagined the brush of leaves across her back when she turned and nothing was there. "I hope so," she said sadly before admitting, "I'm scared." She wasn't sure how long she had been walking when her protesting stomach had her stopping to eat. Unlike last time she had set out, she knew that she needed to make the bread last as long as she could. She didn't want to run out too soon like she had before. She broke off a small piece to eat, and drank her fill of water, draining about a quarter of the jar.

She tried to wish it full again, but it didn't work. The ground was still saturated with water from the storms though and she went over to a nearby puddle and considered her options. The water wasn't exactly clean, but if she couldn't refill the jar, she wouldn't have much choice. The puddle was so shallow that she wouldn't be able to fill the jar directly, so she knelt down next to it and cupped her hands to scoop the water. She noticed that as it pooled in her hands it became crystal clear and she smiled. At least that was something. Maybe that's why she had to leave as soon as the storms ended. So that there would still be water on the ground. It did make her feel better to think so. To know that there was a reason beyond just following an old prophecy. It didn't take her long to fill the jar back up and she replaced it in the bag and pulled the egg sling back over her neck.

When Jaren had first given her the egg, she

wondered if he meant her to eat it, but he told her that it would hatch one day, though he didn't know what would come out of it. Just that she was to care for it. That scared her too. She couldn't even take care of herself. How could she take care of something else? Maybe this guide she was expecting would help. She only hoped that he found her before the egg hatched. Then again, at least if it did she wouldn't be alone anymore. She reached up and rubbed it comfortingly, noticing that, as usual, it warmed at her touch and she smiled. She couldn't shake the impression that it liked her already.

When the sun set that night, she made a bed of leaves, wishing they weren't still so wet, but unable to do anything about it. She chose to look on the bright side; at least they weren't crisp and scratchy. As she lay down, tucking the egg next to her and keeping the horn held tightly in her hand, just in case she needed it in the night, she noticed some movement out of the corner of her eye. She gripped the horn tighter as she turned to look only to breathe a sigh of relief as a large rabbit hopped into her sightline. "Hey little guy. You scared me," she said softly reaching out her hand to see what it would do. She knew that wild animals rarely approached people, so she wasn't expecting much, but sure enough it came over to her and nuzzled her hand for a moment before curling up at her other side, opposite the egg. She grinned as she started to feel some hope that maybe everything actually would be okay. Maybe the forest really was watching over her.

With the egg in the crook of one arm, the rabbit in the crook of the other, and the horn in her hand resting on her chest, she drifted off to sleep.

By this time, the trader had reached the next town, and delivered Jaren's letter to his son along with the warning about the witch in the woods. Arden quickly scanned the letter and wasn't sure what he felt. Sadness that his father was dying, joy that he had gotten his wish of meeting the chosen, jealousy that it hadn't been him who got to meet her, worry for the young chosen. Assuming that she was the witch the trader had warned about, she was barely more than a toddler. He only wished that he could help her. He knew that his father would have done all he could though. He still had to go and see him. He only hoped that he was in time. No one should have to die alone.

He left his shop in his wife's hands and made ready to set out towards the secluded cabin. One of the hunters in the village had no intention of letting him go alone though, knowing that he couldn't shoot to save his life, which may be necessary if they encountered the witch. He tried to fob the man off with excuses, but eventually had to accept that he would have an escort. He knew they would likely not run across her anyway, but if needed, he would do what he had to in order to protect the child and only hoped that it wouldn't spell his own end.

They were three days into their trip before Arden's fears came to fruition as they saw a head of curly hair duck behind a tree. The hunter jumped from his horse and raced after her pulling an arrow from his quiver and drawing back his bow. Arden jumped off his own horse and ran after him, determined to stop him.

It was midday on the second day of her journey when Tiana heard the hoofbeats and hid behind a tree. Unfortunately, she wasn't fast enough. She froze for a moment when she saw the men running towards her but then she started to run away as fast as she could. When she saw the arrow pointed at her, she remembered the horn and put it to her lips and blew, nearly bursting into tears when she didn't hear anything. She felt the sharp pain as the arrow pierced her leg and saw a man tackle the one who shot her and then nothing.

She was surrounded by blackness and she could feel arms wrapped around her torso and the pain in her leg was terrible. She was whimpering, but a hand came up to cover her mouth and a voice whispered in her ear, "I know it hurts kid, but you have to be quiet or they might find us." She nodded and bit her lip hard enough to draw blood in her efforts to say silent and turned her attention to her surroundings to keep her mind off of the pain. At least a little bit. She realized that it wasn't really black. It was just dark and as her eyes adjusted she could both see and feel the hard surfaces pressing against her entire body. She felt like it should hurt, and she shouldn't even be able to breathe, but it felt almost comforting. Aside from her leg and her lip, she wasn't in pain and she was breathing fine. She couldn't move though. It was as if wherever she was had molded itself around her and she wondered how whoever it was that was here with her had moved enough to cover her mouth.

Despite the physical comfort of her position, she could feel the terror clawing at her. She was trapped, unable to move, with someone she didn't know, and she had no idea what was going to happen to her. He seemed to want to help. He had rescued her from the men out there at least, but why? Did he want her for himself or was he like Jaren, just wanting to be kind? That was when a though struck her. Was he the guide she had been waiting for? Oh, how she hoped so. The only way she had been able to cope being alone again was knowing that her guide was coming, and she would never have to be alone after that. That thought allowed the worst of the fear to recede and she no longer felt on the verge of panic, though some still remained and would until she knew what was going on. At least she could still hear what was going on outside.

"Damnit. She got away," the hunter said angrily before rounding on Arden. "What did you think you were doing?"

Now that he knew she was safe, he was able to focus on talking his way out of this without being accused of helping a witch. "I'm sorry. I didn't even realize it was the witch. All I saw was a little girl and didn't think," he said apologetically.

The hunter growled, but accepted the explanation. "And that is exactly why the witch took that form. So that weak-minded people like you would hesitate to do what was necessary."

"I'm sorry," Arden said again. "You're sure she's gone?" He wanted to make sure that he didn't have any clues or tracks to follow.

"Yes. There's nothing here. I saw a demon grab her and they disappeared without a trace. At least I hit her. She should know better than to mess with us again," he said annoyed as he made his way back to where they left the horses.

Arden just shook his head at the man's idiocy. If she really was an 'evil witch rescued by a demon' she would probably come back with a whole army of demons to destroy them for daring to harm her. He kept his mouth shut though, knowing that she was just a little girl with a big job to do and he silently wished her luck as they continued on their journey.

Tiana could hear the hoofbeats fading into the distance and the arms around her tightened once more and pulled her along as they somehow seemed to step through whatever had been holding her in place and she fell to the ground as she turned to see where they had come from as her leg buckled beneath her. "Easy there, kid. Let me see what I can do about that leg of yours."

She finally got a good look at the person...no...creature that was crouching in front of her as he broke the head off the arrow sticking out of her calf. All of her questions evaporated though in the new wave of pain as she cried out as the remainder of the arrow was pulled out and she could no longer hold back the sobs. She didn't even hear the bottom of the old shirt she was wearing rip, but she could feel the cloth being tied tightly around the wound and before she knew it, she was being picked up and the strange being was rubbing her back and whispering comforting words. She couldn't help but soak up the comfort he offered as she wrapped her arms around his neck and buried her head there as she cried. "It's okay, kiddo. I got you. It'll all be okay," he said soothingly rocking her and trying to get her to calm down. He could tell it was as much the stress and adrenaline upsetting her as it was the pain. He continued to talk soothingly and eventually her sobs turned to sniffles as she got herself together.

She started struggling in his arms, so he set her down so that she was sitting against the large tree next to them and crouched in front of her again, so they could talk. "W-what are you?" she asked curiously with just a hint of fear.

"I'm a satyr. My name is Staryn," he told her.

"I'm Tiana. If you're a satyr shouldn't you have curly horns?" she asked skeptically.

He huffed a little in annoyance and pulled his sandy colored hair to the side so that she could see the nubs coming up. "I'm working on it." She started to reach out to touch them but pulled her hand back and looked sheepishly at him. "It's okay. You can touch them," he said encouragingly. He wasn't surprised that she was curious.

"Don't they hurt?" she asked as she lightly brushed her fingers over one of them.

"Nah. They itch like crazy though," he said scratching furiously at them as if to prove his point.

She giggled a little at that before she remembered what had happened and the question that she had been about to ask before the pain overtook her came back to mind. "Were we...inside the tree?" she asked incredulously looking warily over her shoulder as if the tree would swallow her up again.

"Yup," Staryn said with a grin. "That is the oldest tree in the forest. I took you inside it to hide."

She considered that for a moment. "Into its heart," she said thoughtfully.

"You could say that."

"So that's what it meant when it said the ancient of the forest would take me into its heart," she said as much to herself as she did to him.

"You know the prophecies?" he asked hopefully. That would make things easier.

"Yeah. Jaren...he said he was 'the sage' whatever that means...he told me about them and gave me the book. Does that mean you are my guide?" she asked hesitantly.

"That's me," he said proudly puffing out his chest.

"But you're just a kid like me," she protested half-heartedly. She would take whatever company she could get, but she had hoped for a grown-up.

"Hey, I'm not nearly as little as you are," he said defensively. "I was born at the same time as you though," he admitted. "I just age a little faster."

"You were born at the same time?" she asked confused as to how he could possibly know that.

"Mmhmm. When you were born, there was a strong storm before the start of the season. It was a magical storm and while most of the magic went to you, some of it spread out over the land. The forests woke and allowed me to be born. There are probably others too, but I don't know for sure. The elders of the grove taught me all I needed to know to be your guide from that first moment so here we are," he explained.

"Then you know all about all this?" she asked hopefully.

"Not exactly," he said guiltily. "I'm just the guide. I don't have the answers. I'm just supposed to help you find them. And *that* I can do."

Tiana nodded thoughtfully before she pulled her bag around and asked, "Are you hungry?" as she held out some bread in offer.

"What is it?" he asked tilting his head curiously.

"It's bread, silly," she said with a giggle. "Haven't you ever had bread before?"

"No. Is it...good?" he asked hesitantly.

"Uh-huh. It's better with jam though," she told him.

"Jam?"

"Like mashed up berries," she explained.

"Oh! That I can do!" he said happily. "Wait here."

He was gone for about ten minutes and she was starting to worry that he might not come back when he bounded back into the clearing and held out a handful of berries, keeping the other for himself.

Tiana knew that mashing up the berries here would end up wasting a lot so she just popped one in her mouth followed by a small piece of bread and the taste was at least close. The bread wasn't so bland with the berries at least. She giggled again as Staryn made a funny face when he copied her and looked distastefully at the chunk of bread she had given him. "I don't think I like this…bread," he said as he handed it back to her. "I'll just stick with the berries. Thanks though."

They finished their meal and she shared her water with him as well before asking, "Do you know if there's any water nearby?"

"Not really. Other than puddles and stuff of course," he told her.

"Can you take me to the biggest puddle then?" she asked hopefully. With both of them drinking and her not having wanted to fumble in the dark to refill it last night the jar was nearly empty.

He wasn't sure what good a puddle would do, but she was the boss. "Can you walk?" he asked worriedly. She tried to get up, but she couldn't hold her weight on the bad leg. She felt tears of frustration welling up again. How was she supposed to go on a big journey when she couldn't even walk? "Hey now. It's okay. No need to cry. I can carry you," he assured her as he turned around and crouched in front of her. "Climb on."

She shifted the egg to her side instead of her front and climbed on his back, wrapping her arms around his neck and her legs around his waist. He put his hands around her legs for support and bounced her a bit so that she was sitting a little more comfortably and he started walking towards where he had noticed a rather large puddle.

Chapter 5: Magic

It only took a few minutes to reach the puddle that Staryn was aiming for and he set Tiana down on the ground and watched in awe as she reached down and pulled the water from the puddle, cleaning it and placing it in the jar. "Wow," he breathed. He did have some minor powers, most of them relating to the forest, but nothing like that.

She grinned up at him. "I can't make water, but I can clean it."

"And hold it," he pointed out.

"That's not hard. You just have to cup your hands like this," she explained.

The corners of his lips twitched in amusement that she didn't even realize that it didn't work that way, so he set out to show her. He cupped his hands exactly like she was and reached down to pick up some water and it started to run between his fingers and it only took a second for his hands to be nearly empty. "See. That's what usually happens when you try to pick up water like that."

She studied his hands for a minute before she tried again, and sure enough, not a single drop escaped as it turned crystal clear and didn't leave her hands until she poured it into the jar. "Oh," was all she could say to that.

"I bet you could make water. At least when you get older and stronger. If you can control it like that then you probably have a water talent. What else can you do?" he asked curiously.

"Animals like me," she told him. "And once when I got scared, a whole bunch of vines came out of the ground and wrapped around me like a barrier so no one could get at me. I can make water freeze too. And call stuff to me when I can't reach it."

"Sounds like you also have a talent with life too," Staryn told her. He didn't know much about the specifics; that was for her to figure out, but he did know what the different talents were. He wondered if she would find a talent with fire or air as well. Seeing that the jar was full now, he said, "We should probably get a move on. Who knows when those men will come back to this area."

"Okay," she said climbing onto his back again when he crouched in front of her. "Where are we going?"

"The eternal grove where you have to drink from the pools of knowledge. That's the first stop," he told her as he started heading north.

"Then what?" she asked.

"I don't know. You'll find out there where we need to go next."

"How?"

"All I know is that you have to drink from the pool. It'll tell you," he said. When they lapsed into silence he started to ask her questions to make the time go by faster. "So how come you started this whole thing while you're still so little?"

He knew he had asked the wrong thing when he

felt her arms tighten slightly around his neck and heard her start to sniffle. Tiana knew that he should know the story. She shouldn't keep secrets from him. "When the storms started in my village, my papa and I went into town to get some more supplies before they got too bad. A...a sign fell and almost hit papa, but I made it go away, but then it hit someone else and they died. I didn't mean it to!" she added hastily, hoping that he would believe her. "It was an accident, but the people in the village...they were mad. They came to get me, but Papa told me to run away and stayed behind so they wouldn't come after me and they...they killed him," she said as she buried her face in his neck as the tears flowed freely.

Staryn was sorry he asked. "I'm so sorry, Tiana. That must have been scary. It wasn't your fault though. You know that right?"

"I'm the one who moved the sign," she said through her tears.

"Maybe, but like you said. It was an accident. You didn't have a chance to think. You were trying to protect your papa. It's sad that the other person died, but you didn't mean for that to happen and now you know that if that ever happens again to pay more attention to where it's going. That's what matters. That we learn a lesson from our mistakes," Staryn repeated what had always been told to him.

"There...there was a baby too. The lady that died...she had a baby. The baby died too," she admitted.

"Then it's even sadder, but still not your fault," he

said resolutely. "And your papa sounds like a brave man."

"He was the best."

"Tell me about him?" he asked. He had never met a human other than her before. All he'd ever had for company were the trees, so he was curious as to what they were like. That and he thought it might cheer her up to talk about him. It seemed like he was important to her. She obliged him and kept up a litany of stories that kept them both occupied for a while and cheered her up a great deal. It was about an hour that they'd been walking when Staryn suddenly stopped. "Hop down for a minute," he told her and helped her settle on the ground as he walked over to a nearby tree and placed his hand on the trunk. A moment later a few ripe green leaves fluttered down and he caught them from the air and then held them up to the trunk next to his hand. Tiana watched in awe as it seemed like the tree started to bleed but it was yellow and looked really sticky. Staryn coated one side of all the leaves in the sap as he whispered a quiet, "Thank you," to the tree and knelt next to Tiana again.

"What's that?" she asked.

"It will help your leg heal faster and keep you from getting sick from it," he told her as he reached for the bandage.

"How did you make the tree bleed?"

Staryn chuckled a bit as he said, "I just asked for some of its sap...I guess it is kinda like blood, but it doesn't hurt them at all as long as they give it freely.

You can get it by cutting into them, but that's a very mean thing to do."

"You asked it. You can talk to trees?" she asked curiously hissing in pain as he placed the sticky leaves over her wound.

"Sure. The trees raised me. Not the ones here of course, but home…in my grove. They taught me how to talk to them and what kind of trees carried what kind of medicines. I had been looking for the right one since we started walking." He had finished covering the entry and exit wounds and tied the bandage back around to help hold it in place. That done, he crouched down so she could climb on his back again and they started walking once more.

"What are they like?" Tiana asked him.

"Who? The trees?" he asked, and he felt her nod. "They are wise. Strong. They don't like to give straight answers a lot of the time though. They like to make you puzzle it out yourself. They say it makes the mind stronger. They don't usually like humans, because the humans hurt them, cutting off living branches and sometimes cutting off the whole tree, but they like you. They know you're different. You're part of them, just like I am, and all magic is."

"People aren't bad. They don't mean to hurt the trees, I don't think. They just don't know they can feel," Tiana told him.

"Maybe. And that's why the trees don't hurt them in return, but they still don't like them. Now that they're awake though, the older ones can protect themselves.

It's just the younger ones that don't know how that are in the real danger."

"Protect themselves how?" Tiana asked curiously.

"Well they can knock the tools from the people's hands. Or lift their roots and trip them before they get too close. That's enough to scare them away."

Tiana giggled at the thought of people running away from trees and what they must think when the trees fight back. They spent the remainder of the time until they stopped for lunch talking about the trees. Staryn stopped them near a group of berry bushes and started plucking berries, handing some to Tiana and keeping some for himself. He declined when she offered him some bread though. "All you eat is berries?" she asked.

"And nuts and fruits," he told her.

"It doesn't hurt the bush to take the berries?"

"No. Not as long as they are ripe. Once they ripen they start to fall off and it can be pretty uncomfortable until they are loose enough for them to be shaken off, so we're actually doing them a favor by taking the berries. It's less they have to shake off later."

"What about taking the bark and leaves from trees?" she asked. She wanted to make sure she knew what all was okay and what wasn't so she didn't hurt anything on accident.

"The bark that is already falling off is ok, but pulling it off isn't good. Same with the leaves. The ones that die and fall off are fine, but when you pull them off it feels almost like someone pulling out a strand of your hair," he explained.

"That hurts," she said wincing in remembrance.

"Yeah. That's why we only use leaves for healing. They don't mind giving them up for a good cause, but it's always best to ask. They know which ones will hurt the least to remove. The sap too. They know where the closest to the surface is and can bring it out without it hurting."

"But I can't talk to trees like you can," she said biting her lip.

"It's okay. They can still hear you when you talk normally, but if it makes you feel better I can always ask them for you if you need something," he offered.

Once they were moving again, they whiled away the afternoon talking more about the forest in general where Staryn grew up and the village where Tiana did. When the suns started to set, Staryn started looking for a good place to stop for the night and as they ate their berries, Tiana with her bread, Staryn made a suggestion. "How about after we eat, you make us a shelter to sleep in?" He knew that the trees would shield them from any showers that happened by, but part of his job was getting her more comfortable with her powers and exercising them. Besides, if they could take care of themselves they should.

"Make a shelter? How could I do that?" Tiana asked wide-eyed.

"You said that you made vines grow to shield yourself, right? This time just make them grow into a shelter," he suggested.

"I don't know how I did it."

"That's okay. Just try. The only way you'll know what you can do is to try," he prodded gently.

"O-okay. I...I guess I can try," she said nervously. She found a little out of the way area between two trees and held out her hand and concentrated. The vines started to grow up, but when she tried to shape them, they sprung back into the ground and her shoulders slumped. "I can't," she said disappointed. She felt like she was letting Staryn down.

Staryn went and sat behind her and put his hands on her shoulders. "It's okay, Tiana. You almost had it. Just try again. It takes practice. You can't always get it right on the first try. Go ahead," he encouraged her. She lifted her hand and tried again, and the vines started to grow out of the ground. "That's it. You're getting it," Staryn whispered in her ear reassuringly. "Don't force it. Just let it happen. Your magic already knows what to do. Let it go."

Tiana had sweat dripping from her brow by the time she dropped her hand, but there was a shelter there. It was rather lopsided and probably not nearly as waterproof as it could be, but it was there. "I did it!" she said happily.

Staryn hugged her excitedly. "I knew you could do it!" he exclaimed as he rocked her from side to side, unable to stay still. "Come on. Let's get that leg of yours cleaned up and then go to sleep. You're probably even more tired now." She just nodded as she yawned. "As you use it more it won't make you so tired," he assured her as he unwrapped the bandage from her leg. Since he knew she could get more water easily, he didn't worry too much about using what they had to loosen the drying sap from the wound. It would be best to let it breathe tonight and he could find some more medicine for it tomorrow. Once her leg was clean, he carried her over to their shelter and laid down next to her as they fell asleep.

Staryn woke first the next morning and slipped out of the makeshift shelter to start collecting berries for their breakfast but it wasn't long before Tiana woke up too. She was able to use her leg this morning and hobbled out of the shelter and sat down next to one of the trees just as Staryn came over with an armful of berries. Now that Tiana knew that she wouldn't starve when her bread was gone, and knowing that it wouldn't be good forever, she had stopped trying to ration and ate more of it. She was almost finished with the first loaf by the time she was full. She and Staryn did manage to finish the water that was in the jar after what he had used to clean her leg the night before and she got rather nervous when she realized that the ground was nearly dry. "What if there's no more water?"

"There is a small brook about an hour's walk from here. It's not much, but it's still more than a puddle so we'll be able to refill there," he assured her.

"Ok. That's good. But what about after? Or will we be following the brook for a while?" she asked hopefully.

"No. We will just be crossing it, but there will be

more," he said with full faith that the magic would provide, one way or another. It wouldn't let it's chosen down.

While Tiana was now able to hobble short distances, walking all day wouldn't be a good idea, so she climbed on Staryn's back again as they set off, still heading north. When they got to the brook, Tiana climbed down and put the whole jar in the water to fill it up. After she lifted it, before she put the lid back on, she frowned at how murky the water was. Staryn noticed her annoyance and said, "Try dumping it out and filling it with your hands. It's your magic that cleans the water so maybe it has to go through your hands first."

Tiana dumped it out and started picking the water up to put it in the jar and smiled as it worked. The water was just as crystal clear as she was used to. It did take a little longer to fill up that way, but she didn't mind. That done they set off once more, headed for the pools of knowledge.

Staryn was exhausted. It wasn't like walking all day was anything new to him, but carrying someone around while he did had him aching in muscles he never knew he had. He didn't complain though. It was his job to get her where she needed to go, whatever the cost. He would be glad when her leg healed enough for her to be able to walk on her own though.

The next night as they were getting settled for the night, Tiana was getting nervous again. They were out of water and Staryn had said there wasn't any more nearby. Staryn wasn't worried though. He knew that worst case scenario, the trees could save enough of the nightly moisture for them to get by for a few days until they reached the next stream. It would be difficult, but it was possible. When Tiana got their shelter ready, he placed a hand on a nearby tree to ask it for help and the tree told him that there would be showers that night and he breathed a sigh of relief. He relayed the information to Tiana and suggested that they leave the jar out and open tonight so that it could collect the water. The trees would use their leaves to direct it towards the jar.

Then next morning, Tiana was glad to see that they hadn't gotten wet at all. She was getting much better at building the shelters. When she found the jar full, she decided to try something else to clean the water other than dumping it out and refilling it. She put her hand in and stirred it around and sure enough, the water turned crystal clear and she grinned. She should have known that Staryn wouldn't lead her astray. He was her guide after all.

Tiana had noticed that Staryn was having trouble carrying her all the time, so after testing her leg she decided that she would walk today. It was feeling much better. It still hurt, but she could manage. They were moving much slower though. She was naturally slower than him anyway, being so much smaller, but her leg was slowing her down as well. After they stopped for lunch, Staryn did carry her for an hour or so to give her a chance to rest her leg, but she walked the rest of the way.

It was another four days before they reached a large wall. It seemed to be made of vines and Staryn knelt to her level. "Okay so you have to go alone from here," he told her.

"A-alone?" she asked timidly, biting her cheek.

"Just for a while. I'll wait out here for you to return, but only you can enter the clearing."

"You...you won't leave?" she asked hopefully.

"I promise," he said solemnly. "I'll be right here waiting for you, and if you can't find me, then I'll find you."

Tiana nodded bravely. She could do this. She could go alone for a little while and then she could come right back to Staryn. "H-how do I get in?" she asked looking confused at the wall.

"Just make a door. Just like you use the vines for our shelters. It'll close behind you, but you don't need to be afraid," he told her gently.

"O-okay," she stammered nervously and held out her hands, willing a path to appear. When she stepped through she turned to look at Staryn who was giving her an encouraging smile as the doorway closed behind her and he was lost from her sight.

Chapter 6: The Grove

Once she could no longer see Staryn, Tiana took a deep breath and turned around only to have her eyes widen in awe. She had never seen a more beautiful place in her life. Now that she was paying attention, she could feel the grass between her toes as soft as silk, and the small smattering of fruit trees around her carrying fruits that she had never seen before. In her perusal of the area, she saw a small pool in the center of the large clearing, and as hungry as she was, she knew that she was supposed to go straight to the pool and drink. She wasn't sure if she was allowed to eat the fruit, but maybe the pool would tell her.

She quickly made her way over, eager to get this over with and get back to Staryn. As nice as this place was, she didn't really like the idea of being trapped here alone and hoped this wouldn't take too long. After setting her egg next to her, she knelt next to the pool and leaned over, trapping some of the crystal blue water in her hands and brought them to her lips to drink wondering how this would work.

She quickly got her answer as images flowed through her head. First of her sitting there and drinking from the pool and it seemed like time was sped up. She saw many days pass. She would drink and sit for a while before getting up and eating some of the fruit from the trees and returning to the pool for another drink. The images showed her sleeping at night on the soft grass under a nearby tree, and returning to the pool the next morning. Tiana wondered if she had to stay here the whole time or if she could go back out to Staryn for a while, and no sooner than that thought crossed her mind, she saw herself creating a doorway and leaving before turning to enter again, but being unable. She supposed that was the pool's way of telling her that once she left she wouldn't be able to come back. She had to stay here until she had all the answers she needed.

She wasn't sure how long she had been sitting there, but when she came back to herself, she noticed that her hunger had increased exponentially, and the sun was starting to set so she went to the nearest fruit tree and pulled one of the low hanging fruit and put it experimentally to her lips and took a small bite. Her eyes widened in surprise at the taste. She couldn't even decide what it tasted like, it was so different from anything she'd ever had before. The sweetness was pooling in her mouth and just before it got overwhelming, there was suddenly an undercurrent of tartness that cut it just perfectly and she moaned in pleasure. It was the best thing she'd ever tasted in her life. She ate three more of the fruits that were the size of her hand before she curled up under the same tree she had been eating from, egg cradled against her stomach as usual, and promptly fell asleep.

Tiana woke the next morning feeling more rested than she had since leaving Jaren's house. She had needed this rest; this break from the long trek. She ate a few more fruits from the tree before going back to the pool and taking another long drink. This time the images she got were of people she didn't know. There were large groups of people clustered around smaller groups that were doing magic openly. She was getting flashes of magic users causing crops to grow larger and be more plentiful, keep the worst of the storms from ravaging the fields, repair homes and shops that had been damaged, and even heal people who were sick or injured. The images continued for a long time as she saw all the different things that magic was capable of, and how the users helped the people. She could feel the tears welling in her eyes at the idea that these people in the visions accepted magic. They didn't drive them away and try to hurt them. She wanted that. Badly.

She wondered if that image was of the past when magic still lived or what could be in the future if she succeeded. She got the sudden impression that the answer was both, which brought to mind the question of what changed? When had magic become evil? Something to be feared and driven away? She came back to herself before she got an answer to find the twin suns of Linaria high in the sky. She supposed it was time for her midday meal break and she ate quickly before returning to the pool, anxious to get her answers.

This time the images that flowed took on a darker taint. She saw the magic users forcing the people into favors for their help. She saw the people being forced to their knees to worship the magic users as gods. She saw temples and large castles being erected in their honor. She saw the people become little more than servants and slaves. The images showed that some were treated better than others, but that didn't change the fact that they were not in control of themselves. She saw how some of the people tried to fight back, and were quickly struck down. Whole villages were slaughtered when they refused to bow, and Tiana could feel the sobs wracking through her body, even in her dream state, as she watched the carnage.

Her sleep that night was restless and marked by nightmares of blood and death and pain. She knew now why people hated magic and her. She felt dirty, tainted, and she couldn't help but hate them; those old users of magic that twisted it so cruelly. She hated what they had done, and she hated what their actions had done to her. They had cost her her father, her home, nearly even her life and she hated them. When the last nightmare woke her just as the suns were peeking over the horizon, she gave up on trying to sleep anymore, and morosely ate her breakfast and made her way back to the pool, not wanting to see more, but knowing that she had to.

This time, she saw smaller groups of the magic users going back to the ways of before, helping the people for free, and then helping them to rise up against the 'gods' as they were now calling themselves. What followed was a terrible war, involving all manner of magical beings and humans as well as the magicians.

Everyone from the satyrs to the unicorns to the elves, dragons, mermaids, dryads, and even what seemed to be cursed humans in some form of transition between man and beast and just as rabid as any beast could be. All were devastated by the war and the battlefields flowed with blood as the little girl watched on in horror.

When she broke for lunch she wanted even less to go back in again. She just wanted to go home. Home to her father and her village and forget that magic or anything else connected to it ever existed. She wanted to curl up in her father's arms and have these last weeks be just a horrible dream that she would wake up from to find herself safe and loved. Her father was dead though. He wasn't coming back. She would never be in his arms again. She still had Staryn though, and the urge to leave…to go to him and forget all about this place was nearly overwhelming. She was supposed to save the world and she couldn't even comprehend that. All the fears and doubts she had felt when she first learned of her destiny were magnified and she felt so much more lost and alone than she already had.

She didn't even realize that she had spent the entire afternoon lost in her grief until the sun started to set and she was drifting off to sleep. She felt slightly better when she woke the next morning, but not very much so. She managed to eat something since she hadn't eaten since breakfast yesterday, and went hesitantly back to the pool.

Perhaps whatever force was guiding this recognized how close she was to running, or perhaps it was just time for the next part of the story. Whatever the reason, Tiana couldn't help her sigh of relief as the visions started with a man sitting in a familiar house and writing in a familiar book. He was writing the prophecies. She could see the same distant look on his face that she guessed was probably on hers in the real world as he was obviously not seeing anything around him as his quill moved quickly across the page. She saw him place the book and the egg that she now carried everywhere in a hidden cabinet in the bedroom. She saw him call in a young boy, who he proceeded to hug reassuringly and then urge him into the hidden cabinet as well.

That same man was outside in the clearing she recognized so well from her time with Jaren when another man showed up and immediately went on the attack. This battle was just between the two of them and as they both materialized swords she somehow knew that this was the battle that Jaren had mentioned. The one where magic died. These were the last two magicians in the world and she already knew that they were going to kill each other even before the battle reached its end. The one that she thought of as the good magician...the one that wrote the prophecies and protected the boy...got the killing blow against the bad magician, but he was too hurt to move anymore. He fell at the same time and as his blood leaked out onto the ground, his eyes slowly closed for the last time and the ground began to shake.

The next image was of the boy kneeling next to his

body and crying, and then flashed through different scenes of magical creatures, the few that remained after the war, mostly the very young, falling down dead as the groundquakes spread from the spot of their deaths. Every magical creature in the world just ceased to exist when the magic died. The cursed humans woke from their stupors, finding themselves back to normal, and Tiana could almost feel how dead the world was. She could feel the difference even from now, but especially from the rest of what she had experienced.

When magic was at its height, even when they were bad, the world seemed to sing with power, and even now it was there. It was muted and weak, but it was there. After the death of magic though, there was nothing. It was almost like a deafening silence if what was missing had been audible. She knew in that moment that she couldn't let that happen again. That magic had to survive. No matter what she had to do or how hard the journey was. She was filled with a new determination to see it through. She was left with one last image when time seemed to speed past as the twisted black oak grew tall out of the pools of their blood.

When she went back after her midday meal, she found that they were up to more recent history and she found herself in the odd position of watching her own birth. Parts of it anyway, as the scenes flashed by. She saw the off-season storm that hit during the labor and followed the bolts of lightning. One of them hit a tree deep in the forest and as the tree split in two, a little boy came rolling out, and as he stood she recognized him as Staryn. Another bolt of lightning and an obviously pregnant deer gave birth to a dryad. Another bolt and a white mare turned to dust and a unicorn foal stood on wobbly legs, shaking off the dust. A coral reef morphing into a baby kelpie, an elf child formed from a sandstorm, the ocean waves giving birth to a mermaid, the forests beginning to wake, everywhere the lightning touched a new form of magic was born, and Tiana even saw another child...another human child...born of the same magic, but felt the warning inherent in that part of the vision telling her not to look for him yet.

Her dreams that night were nightmare free and filled with the hope and promise of a new world full of magic; of the kind, gentle magic that there used to be. In her dreams she danced with the trees, and played with the other magical children. She swam with the kelpie and the mermaid, and when she woke the next morning she felt ready to continue on her journey. After a hearty breakfast of fruit, she went back to the pool for what she expected to be the last time.

Her visions this time seemed to take two different paths and somehow she knew that one was if she failed and the other if she succeeded. She could feel the waves of uncontrolled magic tearing the world apart as groundquakes and storms far worse than anything the planet had ever experienced ravaged the world. She saw walls of water heading towards the continents to drown them underneath. She saw great plumes of fire and ash shooting towards the sky from the mountains and she knew that if she failed on her quest that would be the outcome. The magic that was born in her and the others would destroy everything.

On the other hand, if she succeeded, she saw a world much like she had first seen in the beginning. One of a symbiotic relationship between the magicians and the people. One where there was peace and harmony and acceptance. If only she knew where to go next; what she was supposed to do to get there. No sooner than she wondered, she received another vision. It was of two great rivers meeting and the churning rapids at their intersection and she was suddenly going beneath the rapids and saw a large red and gold bird struggling against the beating of the water and unable to get free. Once she had processed that image, she received one final vision. She was picking as much fruit as she could carry, even packing it in the sling around her egg, and heading back out of the grove to Staryn.

As Tiana came back to herself, she recognized the dismissal, and was glad that she could get back to Staryn. She couldn't wait for him to try some of this incredible fruit. Maybe he could tell her what it was and where they could find more even. As she turned to leave, she realized that she wasn't sure which way she had come in and where Staryn would be waiting for her. She knew he said that he would find her if they got separated, but she didn't want to wait. She picked a direction that she was hoping was correct, and on the way, she picked as much fruit as she could. When she stepped out the doorway though and looked around...there was nothing. No Staryn, no sign that he had ever been there even, and when she turned to look the other way, she realized that the grove was gone. The vine walls that had been there had disappeared and there was nothing but forest all around.

Chapter 7: Mina

Tiana's father had always told her that if she got lost she should sit and wait for him to find her. Staryn had said that he would find her if she didn't come back. Surely, he had seen the grove disappear too and would be looking. She limped over to the large tree and placed a hand on it as she had seen Staryn do many times and said aloud, "I don't know if you can help me, but maybe you could tell Staryn where I am or help him find me? Please?" This time she knew she wasn't imagining it as one of the branches swung down and trailed it's leaves over her cheek in what she somehow knew what an acceptance of her request. "Thank you," she told him as she sat down to wait.

It had been a long walk out of the grove and her leg was aching, so she took the opportunity to try and massage it out. It was much better than it had been, and she was able to walk mostly normally now, but it still hurt most of the time. She could handle it though. She was almost getting used to it even. She could tell how hard it was for Staryn to carry her all the time, and she didn't want to put more of a burden on him than she had to, so she hadn't told him that her leg still hurt. She was sure that he noticed how she began to limp a bit after a few hours of walking though. He always seemed to stop for a rest or a meal soon afterwards.

It wasn't long after she sat down that she found herself drifting off to sleep. Hopefully, Staryn would find her tomorrow. She was woken the next morning, not by Staryn, but by a muzzle nudging her head. She opened her eyes to find a beautiful silver mare standing over her. At least, what she thought at first was a mare before she wiped the sleep from her eyes and saw the silver horn gleaming on its forehead. "Unicorn," she said in awe, recognizing it from Jaren's stories.

"My name is Mina," she heard a bell-like voice ringing in her head.

"Did you just...talk in my head?" she asked wide-eyed.

"I did. I have never had anyone else talk back to me before. Do you have a name?"

"I'm Tiana," she replied. "No one else can hear you?"

"I have never seen a being like you before, on two legs. Perhaps all of your kind can hear me. I do not know," the unicorn replied.

"What kind of beings have you seen?" Tiana asked as she sat up and offered one of her fruits to Mina, who took it with a nudge of thanks.

"Most have been almost like me. My herd. They did not have the horn, nor were any of them colored like me. They looked at me strangely, but were not unkind. They wouldn't, or couldn't, talk to me though so I set out on my own when I was old enough to find someone that could. I have seen many smaller beings since then, but they all had four legs, and fur on their whole bodies. Why do you only have fur on top of your head?" Mina asked curiously.

"I don't know," Tiana said with a shrug. "All girl humans are that way. Boy humans also have fur on their face after they grow up, but that's all," she explained.

"Strange. How do you keep warm in the cold?" she asked.

"We...um...we wear clothes," she said blushing as she realized that a lot of the way they kept warm outside involved stealing the fur of other animals, and not quite wanting to admit that. "And we use fires."

"Fire?" the unicorn asked, not knowing what that word meant.

"Yeah. It's...um...I'm not sure how to explain it. It makes light and heat though."

"Like the sky orbs?"

"I guess. Kinda. Except it can be made here and doesn't go very far," she explained.

"Can you show me some of this...fire?" Mina asked tilting her head.

"I'm not supposed to use it by myself," she told her. "Staryn, my guide, should be finding me soon and he can show you if you like."

"I think I would like that," Mina replied. "Would you mind if I wait with you? I like having someone to talk to."

"I do too. I don't like being alone," she admitted. "You can travel with us too, if you like. I'm sure Staryn won't mind."

"Perhaps I will. If he doesn't mind," Mina told her as Tiana got up and started to limp towards the nearest puddle. It usually took a few minutes to work the kinks out of her leg when she first got up in the mornings. "You are injured," Mina observed.

"Yeah. It's not so bad, though," she assured her new friend.

"I can see the damage. It is deep. Far below the surface. If you like, I could try to heal it for you," Mina offered.

"You could do that? How?" Tiana asked curiously, making her way back after drinking her fill. She had left her bag and the jar of water with Staryn since she knew she would be able to drink from the pool.

"I don't know. I have healed a few of my herd though when they were injured. I am unsure if it would work on a being such as you, but I could try."

"I would like that. Thank you, Mina," Tiana said gratefully, and the unicorn bowed her head, piercing the arrow wound with the tip of her horn and Tiana hissed a bit in pain, but forced herself to stay still, trusting her new friend not to hurt her. It didn't last long though as she felt the pain starting to fade, even the deep pain that had always been there since she had been shot, and when Mina drew away, Tiana grinned at her. "It worked. It doesn't hurt anymore. Thanks Mina!" she said happily, throwing her arms around the Unicorn's neck.

"I am not familiar with your species, but you seem quite young," Mina asked questioningly.

"Yeah. I'm still just a kid," Tiana confirmed.

"Why is it that you're out here all alone?" Mina

asked.

"I'm not supposed to be alone. I couldn't find Staryn, so I asked the trees to tell him where I am," Tiana told her.

"You can talk to the trees too? I could never get them to talk to me."

"Well I can't hear them, but they can hear me. Staryn can hear them though. They talk to him all the time."

"Staryn is your kin?" Mina asked.

"No. Staryn isn't like me. He's a satyr, but he doesn't have horns yet. They are still growing. He's just my guide. And my best friend," she added.

"I don't believe I have ever met a satyr before either," Mina told her.

"Probably not. He's the only one right now, and I'm sure he would have mentioned meeting you if he had. Plus, he walks on two legs like me, and you said you'd never met anyone with only two legs before. He's really nice though. You'll like him."

"I think I am the only one like me too," Mina said sadly.

"I think so too. I only saw one of you in the visions," Tiana told her.

"Visions?" Mina asked.

"Yeah. I just came from the pools of knowledge in the eternal grove, I think Staryn called it. It showed me stuff from the past and the future. I saw you be born and me and Staryn and lots of other magic people."

"I am…magic?" Mina asked.

"Uh-huh. According to the p-pr-prophecies," she stumbled over the word, "There was no magic in the world until I was born and then it just kinda exploded in a weird storm and lots of us were born at the same time," Tiana explained.

"So, you are as old as me and your species just ages slower," Mina concluded questioningly.

"Yep," Tiana said. "I'm supposed to bring magic all the way back, but I don't know how yet. Staryn said he would help me figure it out though."

"I will help as well," Mina offered.

"Thanks. I think I will need a lot of help."

"Where is your kin? Why do they not help you as well?" Mina asked, wondering why she only spoke of the satyr.

Tiana's face fell. "They died," she said sadly. "My mom when I was born, my dad at the beginning of the last storm season."

"Oh. I'm sorry," Mina said sympathetically. "Were you along long after?" she remembered Tiana's statement about not liking to be alone.

"Yeah. A lot. For lots of days before I found Jaren, and then even more before Staryn found me," she said as she launched into the tale of what happened since she started her journey, leaving out the events of the village that got her started.

"That is quite the tale. A great burden for one so young," Mina said when Tiana finished.

"But I'm not alone anymore," Tiana said cheerfully, shaking off the sorrow. "I have you now, and soon

Staryn will be back and then we'll be three."

"I hope he will be able to talk to me too," Mina said wistfully. She had been so alone for so long. Having two people to talk to would practically be heaven for the lonely unicorn.

"I bet he will. He talks just like me and we're all the same; we're all magic, so I bet he can talk to you," Tiana assured her.

"Will you tell me about your people?" Mina asked, curious about what they were like, but mostly just wanting to hear someone talk to her.

The whiled away the next few hours in conversation about humans and how they lived, but Tiana avoided any talk about what had happened in the village that sent her out here. Some of the concepts took a bit of time to explain to Mina, like homes and schools and shops, and even currency. Tiana struggled to try and explain them, but it passed the time.

Tiana was just getting ready to pull out some more fruit for lunch when she heard footsteps. She jumped to her feet and hid behind a tree, watching to see who it was before she cried, "Staryn!" and ran towards him, jumping into his arms.

"There you are kiddo. I was worried about you. You doing okay?" He asked as he set her down and looked her over. He knew how much she hated being alone. He had noticed how tense she got even when he just went foraging for berries and he was never gone for more than a few minutes.

"Uh-huh. I made a new friend. She's a unicorn. Her

name is Mina. Come meet her," she babbled excitedly.

"A unicorn? Really? That's great!" Staryn said following her back over where Mina was waiting nervously.

"Hi, Mina. I'm Staryn," he introduced himself.

"Hello Staryn," she said, waiting with trepidation to see if he had heard her.

"You talked in my head! That's amazing," he told her. "Do you want to travel with us?"

"I would like that very much," Mina said tossing her head happily.

"She's never found anyone who could talk to her before. She's been really lonely like I was," Tiana told Staryn.

"Well now you have us, so you don't have to be lonely anymore," Staryn addressed his reply to the cheerful unicorn.

"She even healed my leg for me. Look," Tiana told him, proudly showing off her unblemished skin. "It doesn't even hurt a little bit anymore."

"That's great! Thank you, Mina," Staryn said reaching out to run a hand down her neck before turning back to Tiana. "So, what did you learn in the grove?" he asked. "Do you know where we are supposed to go next?"

"Uh-huh. I have to go find a pretty bird. He's trapped in the water that spins around," Tiana told him.

"Water that spins around?" Staryn asked as he thought about that trying to figure out where it could be. He had been drilled nearly constantly on every inch of their continent, and quite a bit of the other continents in the world. The grove had been reasonably certain that Tiana's journey wouldn't take her off of this continent, but they thought it best to be prepared just in case. "I wonder if that means the meeting of the great rivers," he pondered.

"I think so," Tiana told him. She remembered seeing two rivers in the vision.

"Okay. I know where that is. Why don't we have lunch first and you can tell me about what else you learned before we can start heading that way," he suggested.

"Okay," Tiana told him before handing him a fruit. "What kind of fruit is this? It's the best thing in the world," she asked.

"I don't know," Staryn said turning it over in his hand. "I've never seen one before. Let me see if I can find out." He placed a hand on the nearest tree and closed his eyes for a moment as the tree answered his question. "It was called a Joramberry. They don't grow anymore though. They all died a very long time ago. You found it in the eternal grove?"

"Uh-huh. There were lots of trees with them. I brought back as many as I could carry," she told him.

"Well if you like them so much, you should keep them since we'll never find anymore," he told her handing it back to her.

"Uh-uh. I brought it for you," she told him. "You have to try them too. They are the best. I wonder if we could plant some of the seeds in it and see if it will grow more again."

"Even if it works it will be years before they are growing fruit," Staryn told her, still waiting for her to take it back.

"That's okay. I still want you to have some," Tiana told him and Staryn realized that she wasn't going to take no for an answer.

He took a bite of the fruit and managed to keep his face schooled. She was right about them being the best. He had never tasted anything like it. He wasn't going to tell her that. "I don't know. It's a little too sweet for me. You have it. I'll get some of the regular berries."

This time she did take it back. "You really don't like it?" she asked even more confusedly than she had when she realized that he didn't like bread. When he shook his head, she did the same as she said, "You're weird."

Staryn chuckled a bit and ruffled her hair. "Right back atcha, kid."

"Do you want another one?" Tiana asked Mina, who realized what Staryn had done and decided to do the same.

"They are a bit too sweet for my taste as well," she told her. "Thank you though."

Tiana just shrugged and finished the one that Staryn had tried. By the time she finished her first, Staryn was back with berries for himself and shared some with Mina as well as Tiana ate a second fruit and started her story from the grove. "I saw lots of other magic people like us being born," she started. "Some lived in water and some in the woods. One even lived in the desert. Do you think I will find them too?" she asked.

"Probably," Staryn told her.

"I agree," Mina said. "I found you because I felt drawn to you. I would guess that the others would feel the same if we get close to them."

"Good," Tiana said with a smile. She saw the magical beings as her new family and wanted to find as many of them as she could. "The water also told me what happened with magic before and how it died." When Staryn looked at her curiously she started the story. "Back in the beginning the magic users were nice and they helped people and stuff. Then they started getting mean and started making people do stuff before they would help, even making them do bad things and they started hurting and killing anyone who wouldn't. Then the nice magicians tried to help and there was lots of killing until the last two magicians killed each other and then magic died everywhere, and that's why people are so scared of me and of magic now."

"Well we know that you would never be like that," Staryn told her. "I can't believe that they didn't. You're like the good magicians."

"I hope so," Tiana said worriedly. The bad ones were good before too. What if she became bad someday.

"I know so," Staryn told her, putting a hand on her shoulder.

"So, do I," Mina chimed in. "I have not known you for long, but I knew as soon as I saw you that you could never be evil. You don't have it in you."

Tiana managed a slightly confident smile. "I'm glad," she said, hoping that they were right.

"Did you learn anything else about what you have to do to fix magic?" Staryn asked.

"No. I think I'm still supposed to figure that out myself. I did learn more about what I could do, though. And it showed me what will happen if I can't do it, and what the world will be like if I do."

"That's good," Staryn told her. "You probably won't be able to do everything until you get older and stronger, but at least now you know what to work towards." He could tell her all day long, but until she could see it and feel it, it wouldn't be real to her, so he was glad she had that reference now. "Well we should get moving. It will be a few weeks walk to the meeting of the great rivers."

Chapter 8: Hunters

Tiana and Staryn walked through the forest in the direction Staryn indicated. The satyr would check his way each hour with the trees to ensure they hadn't wandered off course. Mina walked beside them, slowing her steps so as not to get too far ahead. It wasn't until they had stopped for the night that she realized that they were different in more than the fact that they had fewer legs. "You are fatigued," she observed curiously.

"Yes. A lot of walking makes us tired. Especially our legs," Tiana told her.

Mina didn't say anything but found herself lost in thought so much that she didn't even join in the conversation between Tiana and Staryn as the three of them ate dinner. After dinner, Tiana sat cross-legged on the ground and began the well-rehearsed routine as she slowly called the vines from the ground and weaved them together to create a small shelter from the storm for herself and Staryn. She had gotten much better at it, and her shelters were much more sturdy and hardly leaked at all anymore. Once she and Staryn had a shelter made she turned to Mina. "Where would you like to lay?"

"Oh, I don't lay," Mina told her. "I sleep standing up."

"You do?" Staryn asked curiously. "Isn't that

uncomfortable?"

"Not for me. I would imagine lying down would be quite uncomfortable for me."

"Okay, how about something like this then," Tiana suggested as her hands began to dance in the air as if crafting the hutch with her fingers rather than her magic and a tall narrow shelter grew up from the ground. Mina was about to tell Tiana that she didn't need a shelter and had never had one before but Staryn shook his head at her, and she understood. The more Tiana could exercise her powers, the more she used them, and learned to make them second nature, the better they all would be, so she allowed the little girl to build her a shelter and even stepped inside it to sleep as the suns disappeared beyond the horizon.

Staryn gave her a grateful nod as he climbed into his own shelter, waiting for Tiana to join him before he pulled her back tightly against his chest while she cradled her egg to her own chest and they settled to sleep in the long-familiar position. The next morning, once Tiana had filled her water jar and Staryn had collected his berries, they sat down for breakfast. As they ate, Mina told them her idea. "Perhaps if the two of you rode on my back we would make better time and you would be less fatigued."

Mina had never been near a village to know that humans often rode horses. Tiana was the only one that had, but she would never have brought up the idea of riding her new friend. Horses were animals. Mina was not. Mina was people. "Are you sure you don't mind?"

she asked worriedly.

"I am certain," Mina told her. "If it is uncomfortable for me we do not have to continue the arrangement, but it is worth the attempt. My legs do not tire, after all."

"That would be very kind of you, Mina," Tiana told her. "Thank you. But you have to promise that if you don't like it, you let us know. You're our friend first."

"I will do so," Mina promised. Staryn had stayed out of the conversation, not having familiarity with the practice like Tiana or having any idea of Mina's capabilities. Once it was decided though, he had to admit that he was happy to have a chance to rest his legs, even would turn out to be short-lived.

Once they had finished their breakfast and drank their fill, Staryn first lifted Tiana to Mina's back and only after making sure that she was comfortable, did he climb up himself and they set off. The pace was only marginally faster than they could walk, though Mina assured them that if the need arose she could run with great speed, but doing so would cause her fatigue, so they walked at what for the unicorn was a leisurely pace, but they would have been walking quite briskly, or perhaps even jogging to match.

Mina had long since gotten used to grazing without stopping, as long as she was walking slowly enough, as she was here, so when they suggested stopping for lunch, she told them that they were welcome to eat as they were if they liked, but she had no need to stop. By the time they stopped as the suns started to set though, both of the humanoids decided never to do that again. Even Mina couldn't help but laugh at the funny way they walked as they gathered their dinner and began to settle in for the night.

After that, the remainder of the journey was spent with them riding in the afternoons, but walking in the mornings. That allowed them to work out all the kinks in their muscles and joints, both from sleeping and from the previous days ride, during the morning, and then ride in the afternoons, once they were starting to get tired. It worked very well that way, and they found their pace increased greatly.

It wasn't until nearly a week into their journey that they were even more grateful for Mina's addition to their numbers as they were spotted by a group of hunters. Word of the little 'witch' had spread far and wide by this point, and Staryn's appearance with the lower body of a goat and the horns which were just starting to peak above his sandy hair did not help matters. The three of them had been so deep in conversation, letting down their guard due to the peace of their recent journey, that even Staryn had missed the whispered warnings of the trees until they were right on top of the hunters.

It was lucky for them that the hunters froze for a moment, as so did Staryn while his mind worked frantically through possible escape plans. Taking her into the trees wouldn't work again. Not here, and not only because they were close enough to see which tree they entered and easily surround it and either cut it down or wait them out. There was also the fact that he wouldn't be able to take Mina with him, so she would be left on her own and could be captured or killed and that was not an option at all. It wasn't until he heard Mina's bell-like voice ringing in his head, "Get on! Both of you!" that he realized that he had missed the obvious escape.

It had only been a few seconds but felt like minutes before Staryn grabbed Tiana and practically threw her on the unicorn's back before jumping up after her just as the hunters shook off their stupor and they heard one of them exclaim, "It's the witch and the demon!" and Mina picked up speed as they heard the sound of hoofbeats behind them.

Staryn knew that despite Mina's speed, they were not fast enough to lose their pursuers, and he knew of nowhere they could hide with the unicorn, so there was only one other option. "Mina, can you keep us as steady as you can?" Staryn raised his voice over the rushing wind. When he heard the answering acceptance in his mind, he waited until the ride steadied off, though they had lost a bit of speed, but that was unavoidable, and hopefully wouldn't matter for long. He wrapped his arms around Tiana and turned them as easily as he could, nearly falling off as he did, but he felt Mina shift underneath them enough that he was able to counter their balance and get them resettled, now facing backwards. "Okay, Tia. Do you think you can slow them down?" Staryn asked.

"H-how," Tiana asked fighting back her panic and

tears.

"Why not a wall of vines, like was at the grove. We know you're good at vines. Or you can crack the ground so they can't pass. Or...I don't know...something else," Staryn was at a loss of what else to suggest. She was still unable to create water so she would have to work with what they had.

Tiana bit her lip as she tried to think fast. She could see the hunters gaining on them and knew she didn't have long. She knew that cracking the ground would be faster, but if she did that then they and their horses might fall and get hurt if they couldn't stop fast enough. She remembered what Staryn had told her about learning from her mistakes and hurting someone was not a mistake she intended to make again. They might still get hurt if they ran into the wall, but it probably wouldn't be too bad. She came to the conclusion and began to build the wall of vines in their path, but they jumped right over it and she felt the tears welling up in her eyes as the fear ramped up higher.

"It's okay Tia," Staryn said soothingly, forcing his own fear back in order to help her. "Just close your eyes and see the wall you started in your mind. Make it bigger and wider. You don't have to be next to it. You just have to picture it," he really hoped he was right about that. "You do that and we'll circle back around. Leave a little hole for us to get through and then seal it behind us okay?" Staryn suggested calmly.

Tiana swallowed hard around the lump in her throat and nodded so Staryn turned behind him. "Are you okay to keep this up for a little longer, Mina?" he yelled to her.

"I will be well for a while yet," she told him. She would need to rest by the time this was all over, but she would not let herself falter while her only friends and, dare she say, family, were in danger. She would push herself as hard as was necessary to save them, and herself. Especially since she had learned in that brief encounter that she could not speak to them. They had showed no response whatsoever to her words of peaceful warning. She was no more than her kin to these speechless two-legs and she would have to do battle on that level were they to get out of this mess. She began a large circle, noticing the hunters continuing to follow and she saw the wall as soon as she broke through the nearby trees and she picked up her speed as she saw a hole opening to allow them passage.

Staryn was holding tightly to Tiana, still facing to the back and leaving Mina to the navigation as he whispered encouragement into her ear as her hands danced in front of her. The wall may have been technically behind them at this moment, but she was still seeing it in her mind in front of her, even as she could sense the power heading behind her and she knew they were close. What happened next was a combination of many factors. Mina's increase in speed when she saw the opening forming. Tiana's failure to take that into consideration. Staryn's curiosity that had him lifting his head to turn it at just the wrong time to allow one of his horns to catch on the top of the little opening that Tiana had made them.

Staryn was jerked off the unicorn pulling Tiana with him and Mina skidded to a stop as she turned to see what had happened to them just in time to see a large tree step in the way of the opening. She almost wondered if it was Tiana's doing, having never seen a tree move on its own before, but then she realized that Tiana was not in any condition to be doing anything right now as she bent over the young Satyr, sobbing. The young satyr that was far too still. Even in sleep he was never so still, and the unicorn felt her heart drop as deep as the child's clutching him. It wasn't until she began to walk over that Tiana looked up, tears streaming down her cheeks. "C-Can you...h-heal him?" she asked with a heart-breaking hope.

"I don't know," Mina told her. "I don't think so. Not all the way," she said as some part of her mind instinctually scanned and categorized his injuries.

"Please Mina...y-you have to...to save him...p-please," Tiana sobbed. She could feel his spark dimming. She could feel the magic fading from his body as he began to slip away. She knew what that meant, and she couldn't let it happen. Not to Staryn. Not now. He was her best friend. He was her savior, her guide, her confidante, her everything. She had lost so much, and she knew, in that moment, that this loss would break her. For good. She couldn't let this happen.

Mina too could see it. The light fading from the satyr, and from the eyes of the chosen, and she too knew that the fate of the entire world rested on the life of this one little Satyr and she would do whatever she could to make sure that the worst did not happen here. She couldn't heal him all the way, but she could help. Hopefully enough to allow him to live long enough for her to teach Tiana to heal. She had far more power than Mina could ever hope to have. Mina lowered her head and used her horn to pierce the skin at the base of Staryn's neck where the worst of the damage was centered.

It was only a few moments before she could feel the fatigue setting in due to both the running and the healing and she stepped back. That was the cue for Tiana to put a hand on Staryn's shoulder and give it a small shake. "Staryn. Wake up, Staryn…He won't wake up," she cried looking up at Mina, begging with her eyes to do something.

"I know. I could not do much. His injuries are quite severe. You can see he is no longer fading though. You are more powerful than I. Perhaps I can teach you to heal so that you can finish healing him. In the meantime, he will not die, but he will not wake either," she told her. About that time, they were able to hear pounding and voices from the other side of the wall. "How thick is this wall?"

"I don't know," Tiana asked worriedly. "What do we do?" she started to panic. It was usually Staryn who made the plans. It was his job. She had no idea where to start, but she did know that the people on the other side of that wall were trying to come through. Perhaps they had seen Staryn fall and thought that they would be stopped to care for him rather than still running where they couldn't hope to catch up.

"We have to keep moving," Mina said tiredly.

"We're not leaving Staryn," Tiana said harshly.

"I would never have suggested it, child," Mina assured her soothingly. "Perhaps you can grow the vines beneath him into a carrier of sorts and loop it around my body, so we can pull him behind me."

Tiana didn't know if she had the strength to keep using her powers, but there wasn't a force in the world who was going to stop her from doing it anyway. If Staryn were awake he would tell her to be careful. To not push herself so far. If Staryn were awake, she wouldn't need to, and she would do anything to save him. She knew that if those hunters came through before they were ready she wouldn't even hesitate to do whatever must be done. If she had done that to begin with, they wouldn't be in this situation. If she had just cracked the ground behind them to stop them from following, Staryn wouldn't be hurt. She could feel herself being drawn down a dark hole even as her powers flowed from her fingers, lifting Staryn from the ground.

Mina could feel the darkness beginning to swirl around the child, and it frightened her greatly. She wasn't sure why. She wasn't frightened of Tiana. At least she didn't think she was, but the power clinging to her now, terrified her. She could see that the anger and the fear was the only thing pushing the girl now and didn't dare interrupt her. She only hoped that this dark power didn't interfere with Tiana's ability to heal later. It felt very hostile to whatever part of her being did the healing.

Tiana fashioned the carrier as something between a cart and a plow as she had seen them. It was low to the ground and had just a small platform where Staryn was now laying, but rather than spikes to plow the soil, it had round viney wheels like a cart would. The harness that went over Mina's neck was also modeled off of the yoke of a plow, and once she was done, the girl lay next to the Satyr and closed her eyes, drifting off into nightmares as Mina pulled them deeper into the forest.

The unicorn had no way of knowing whether they were going the right way to Tiana's next stop, but at the moment she hardly cared. She only cared about putting some distance between them and the speechless ones. Enough distance that she too could rest. She didn't notice the tracks left by the makeshift cart, nor did she notice the way the wind picked up in their wake, removing the tracks nearly as soon as they formed while the young chosen and her guide slept on.

Chapter 9: Depression

Mina trotted through the woods, making sure to stay in the same direction she started in, in order to put as much distance between them as possible before she just couldn't possibly go on any longer. She had no idea how to unhook this harness from her neck, but it wasn't overly uncomfortable anyway. Not as exhausted as she was. She worried briefly for the two younglings out in the open rather than under their usual shelter, but there was little she could do about it, save waking Tiana up, and she didn't dare. Nor could she muster up the energy to care for more than a moment before sleep claimed her.

Tiana was the first to wake in the morning, just as Linaria's suns were starting to peek over the horizon. She had slept for half the day and the full night. It wasn't until she was sitting up, rubbing the sleep from her eyes, that she remembered what had happened yesterday and her eyes snapped open the remainder of the way and she spun to look at Staryn. "Staryn! Wake up, Staryn!" she whispered loudly, trying not to wake Mina and feeling the tears welling up in her eyes at his continued silence and eerie stillness. "Please, Staryn," she wept as she leaned her head down onto his chest. "Please don't go," she whispered softly, willing her powers to do something. Anything. What good were they if they couldn't even heal her guide?

Part of Tiana knew that it was hopeless though. If healing was that easy, if she could heal at all, she would never have had to suffer through the burn in her hand for days. She would never have had to suffer the wound to her leg for weeks. But Mina had said...she'd said that she might be able to teach her to heal. She had to force herself not to wake the unicorn up to get started. Only the fact that she was unsure how far she had run while Tiana herself was sleeping kept her from doing just that. She had likely pushed herself as hard as she possibly could, and deserved her own chance to recuperate. As long as Staryn would survive that long, she added to herself as she continued to weep on his shoulder, not willing to let him go. Not even for a moment. At least she could see the truth in Mina's words. Staryn was no longer fading.

Tiana still had not moved, not even for food, by midday when Mina finally woke. Tiana didn't notice though until she heard the voice echoing in her head, "How is he?"

"He still won't wake up," Tiana sobbed heartbrokenly. She was so lost without him. She didn't know where to go or what to do.

"But he is still living?" Mina asked.

Tiana nodded before realizing that Mina couldn't see her, and she sniffed out a quiet, "Uh-huh."

"If you can release me from this carrier, I can look him over as well and see if there is any more I can do, now that I'm rested," Mina offered.

Tiana absently waved her hand, not even noticing how easily the magic flowed through her as the harness unsnapped from Mina's neck and the unicorn turned to look at them. "He is gaining strength, but you are losing it. You have not eaten, have you?" Mina asked worriedly.

"I'm not hungry," Tiana grumbled.

"Regardless, you need to eat. If you are going to have any hope of healing him, you will need your strength." Tiana bit her lip worriedly as she released her grip on Staryn enough to look back towards the woods and then back to him. "Go on, child. I will keep watch over him until you return."

Tiana reluctantly pulled herself off of the cart and scampered into the woods, intending to be back as quickly as possible as she hunted down the nearest berry bush, taking back as many berries as she could carry, partially so that she wouldn't have to leave Staryn again until he woke, but mainly so that he would have some if he did. She rushed back to his side, taking a handful of the berries for herself, and saving the rest for later. For him, hopefully. No sooner than she lay down curled up to his side once she finished eating, Mina suggested, "Perhaps, if you are feeling well enough, you should build a shelter. We may be staying put for a while so perhaps something larger and more long term for him to recover in?"

Tiana sighed, knowing that Mina was right, so she sat back up, still not going far as she began to build right around them. She rose the walls high above her head, and turned the cart that Staryn was resting on into a bed of sorts before she rushed out the door she had created and grabbed a chuck of moss off of a nearby tree. She returned into the make-shift house and set the moss on the 'bed' and put her hands on it. While she still couldn't quite manage to create water yet, but Staryn had taught her enough about life that she could create moss. Or more like, she could increase the growth rate of the moss to allow it to cover a larger surface, even allowing it to grow underneath Staryn so that he would have a more comfortable place to lay.

Mina had stepped away as the walls started growing. She didn't much like being surrounded on all sides by anything. Even her shelters that Tiana usually built her had little more than a roof held up by poles, after she made the request for such. She did notice that Tiana left a large open window. Large enough for her to push her head in and check on them or even sleep like that if she chose which she likely would. She worried greatly about little Tiana. Even now she could see her spark dimming as the darkness pulled her in deeper. She only hoped that her guide would wake soon and pull her back to the right path. Even Mina knew how wrong this was, but she had no idea what to do. Hopefully he would wake before she had no choice but to figure it out.

Tiana only stepped outside of their little hut once more before the suns set and that was only to place the jar of water outside. She was hoping that it would rain tonight so that she wouldn't have to go searching for water. It was still half-full, given that only one had been drinking from it, but she needed to make sure there was enough for Staryn when he woke up. When that was done, she climbed up in the bed she'd made and cuddled up to Staryn's side as she slept fitfully, plagued by nightmares of fear and pain and darkness. Nightmares of the end of the world. Of her parent's disappointed faces. Of Jaren's disappointed face. When she woke, all she could remember of them was the helplessness. None of the faces. None of the warnings. She turned her head and sobbed into Staryn's shoulder as she realized that he still wasn't awake yet.

She forced herself to eat another handful of berries as she turned to look at Mina waiting for her to wake up too. She needed to start learning healing today. She should have yesterday, but she had been so tired after building this hut and still wasn't fully recovered from the chase, but she couldn't put it off any longer. She had to learn this. She had to do her part to help him. It wasn't long before Mina's eyes opened and met the child's purple gaze. "I assume you wish to begin learning to heal," Mina guessed at the expectant look.

"Yes, please," she said quickly.

"Alright. Sit up and make yourself comfortable," Mina told her. It would be difficult to explain in such a way that Tiana could understand, but she would do her best. "Now close your eyes and just center yourself." Tiana scrunched up her nose in confusion, so Mina tried again. "Just...let all your troubles float away. No fear. No worry. No anger. Just peace."

"How can I do that when Staryn is...like this?" Tiana asked bitterly.

"Only when you find a way can you hope to heal him," Mina told her, as concerned at the tone of her words as by everything else that had gone wrong since the start of this incident. "Only when the heart and mind is truly at peace can the healing power be released."

"I...I don't think I can," Tiana said with a sniffle.

"It's alright, child," Mina told her. "It takes time. It's not something you will get right away. The more you try the better you will get, so why don't you just sit there for a while and keep trying." If nothing else, it would give her something to do other than cry. When Tiana nodded, she pulled her head from the window and went to look for her own food and water.

"I'm s-sorry, Staryn," Tiana whispered through her tears. "I want to heal you, but I'm just not good enough. I just can't and I'm sorry. I...I should have made the hole bigger. I...It's my fault you're hurt. It's my fault I can't heal you. I-if you die, t-that'll be my fault too. I-I'm sorry Staryn. S-so sorry." It took a few minutes for her to pull herself together enough to do as Mina had suggested and began to try and let everything go. It wasn't very long before she was pulled from her efforts by the sound of a soft groan. "STARYN!" Tiana cried out before hopping off the bed and grabbing for the water, figuring he would be terribly thirsty by now. "MINA! COME QUICK!" she yelled as she did so and rushed back to Staryn. "Here's some water, Staryn." He still didn't reach for it though, or make any move to sit up despite his eyes being open. He wasn't even looking at her. "S-Staryn?" she asked shakily.

"I can't move," he croaked out. "O-or see." He was doing his best to tamp down the pure panic he felt rolling through him.

It was a good thing he couldn't see Tiana's eyes go wide or the tears that started pouring down her cheeks at that, but somehow the little girl was able to keep her voice mostly steady as she told him, "Okay. I'll help you. It's okay," she said as though she were trying to will herself to believe it as she climbed up on the bed next to him and moved so that his head was resting in her lap. "Let's have some water first. You've been out for a while and you're probably really thirsty," she said, trying to keep talking to keep herself calm, not even realizing that with him not being able to see, it was helping Staryn just as much as it was her. She tilted the jar of water to his lips as he began to drink. For a moment at least and then he started to choke, and she jerked the jar away and tried to push him up farther, but mostly failed. The choking fit did pass momentarily though. "I'm sorry," she sniffled.

"S'okay. Just...not so fast?" he said trying to be reassuring, but not particularly in the mood.

"Okay. Sorry," Tiana said again as she put the jar to his lips again, tipping it into his mouth slowly this time until he turned his head away. "You're not thirsty anymore? That's okay. How about some berries? I saved you a lot. I bet you're really hungry."

"I'm not hungry," Staryn said emotionlessly, the full weight of the current situation starting to bear down on him.

"Please, Staryn? Eat *some* at least?" Mina cut in, seeing that Tiana was about to take his words at face value, likely not even considering the idea that Staryn would lie to her. Unfortunately, she wouldn't be able to take care of him. That job would have to be left to Tiana, but that didn't mean she couldn't do anything.

"If I must," Staryn said with a sigh and Tiana grabbed some and plopped them in his mouth one at a time, having learned from the issue with the water, as he slowly chewed and swallowed. He managed to eat a full handful before he refused to take anymore.

"Do you want to do anything?" Tiana asked not really sure what to do with herself now. "I could try to sit you up for a while if you feel up to it. Or I could tell you a story. Or you could tell me one. Or maybe Mina could even tell us a story. I made us a little house here, so we can stay for a while until you're better. Don't worry. We'll take care of everything, Mina and me. So, what do you want to do?" she finished, only to get no response. "Staryn?"

"I just want to rest," he said distantly and Tiana bit her lip and nodded before remembering he couldn't see her.

"Okay. I'll let you rest. But I'll be right here if you need anything," she promised.

"You don't have to," he told her. "You shouldn't have to take care of me. I'm not meant to be your burden," he whispered too softly for her to hear as a single tear made its way from his eye and he hoped that Tiana had already moved far enough away that she wouldn't see it.

Tiana spent most of the remainder of the day trying to meditate as Mina had told her. The next day was very much like this one. Staryn would eat and drink when prompted, but rarely spoke, and only wanted to rest, but Tiana noticed that he wasn't sleeping. His eyes were open, staring at nothing, occasionally leaking tears, but that was it. There were no other signs of life from the young Satyr.

It was nearly a week before Tiana was at the end of her rope and Mina couldn't really do much with her at all. Tiana didn't mind taking care of Staryn. He had done so much to take care of her after all, it was only fair. That wasn't what she was having trouble with. No, her trouble was with Staryn's attitude. Or lack of one, and she only had one idea left. She stepped outside, tempted to slap herself for not thinking of this sooner and walked over to the nearest large tree she could see. She put a hand flat on the trunk and said, "I need your help. Please. It's Staryn. He's been hurt really bad, and I'm scared. He...he won't talk or eat. It's like he just...doesn't want to live anymore and I...I can't help him," she sniffled. "I tried, but I can't, and I know you're his family too and I hoped...maybe you could."

She got her answer in a small branch brushing down her cheek before a long branch reached towards her makeshift window, Mina hustling out of its way, and reached in before pulling Staryn out, having wrapped around him and Staryn disappeared into the trunk of the tree. Into its heart, Tiana still called it. Hopefully he could be helped there. They could help his heart, and Tiana would redouble her efforts to help his body. While he was in the tree, she sat and tried once more to meditate. She had gotten close a few times, but hadn't quite gotten there yet.

Staryn felt a paralyzing fear grip his body as he felt himself suddenly lifted off the bed without a word. It wasn't until he felt the branch strongly supporting the back of his head and the leaves brushing over his cheek that he realized that one of the trees was carrying him. They were taking him home. He would miss Tiana, but she would get a new guide, now. A whole one. She had to. "She will not," he heard a voice that he recognized as the tree.

"S-she will not, what?" Staryn asked.

"She will not get a new guide, young Staryn. You are the only guide, and you will continue to guide her or the world is lost."

"But...how can I guide her like this," Staryn protested. "I can't even see. I can't move. I...I'm nothing anymore," he finished sadly.

"You still have use of the most important part of you, Staryn. Your heart. You see, you were not meant to only guide her steps. You are meant to guide her heart as well. You can learn to navigate in the dark. Just as you did as a sproutling with the less complete darkness of night. Your way to her heart is unimpeded and more important than ever," the tree told him seriously.

"What do you mean?" Staryn asked worriedly.

"She carries a darkness inside her now. One that threatens to consume her if you are not careful. You *must* bring her back, and soon. The quest must start again. Within the next few cycles. There is little time to waste. You are still more than capable of your duty, young one. And it is more crucial than ever before that you stay the course."

"So, I'm just stuck like this forever?" Staryn asked fighting the urge to sob.

"The future is unclear," the tree told him. "The world is currently at a crucial junction. There are many paths leading from this point. Some of those paths do have you walking and seeing again. Some show your death in the very near future. All of our fates hinge on the chosen child, and only you can reach her. Do not fail us, Staryn. Please."

Chapter 10: Darkness

With those words, Staryn found himself pulled from the comfort of the tree's core, and was placed gently back in the soft bed that he was in before, finally noticing that it was softer than anything else they'd ever had. "Tiana?" he asked wondering if she was nearby.

"I'm here, Staryn," he heard rushing footsteps and the quiver in her voice and nearly winced at the thought of what his melancholy must have done to her, even without the fact that she was likely to be blaming herself anyway. They had a lot to talk about.

"Where are we?" he asked curiously first.

"I'm not sure exactly where we are. Mina just ran us that day until she got too tired," Tiana said regretfully. "I know there is a small stream in the direction the moss grows. It's about as wide as my arm and as deep as my ankles. There is a big group of berry bushes in the direction the suns set, that have three different types of berries and Mina found a large clearing in the direction the suns rise."

"Does the clearing have a large redwood tree in the center?" Staryn asked trying to get his bearings.

"Uh-huh," Tiana told him, hoping she had been able to help.

"Okay. Then I know where we are. We are pretty far off course, but we can get back on track. How far is the clearing?" he asked. If he could get a chance to talk to the old redwood before they left he would gladly take it, but he wouldn't push their schedule back for it. The old redwood was something of a legend though. One of the eldest of all the trees and the only one any of them had heard of who was a hermit. Trees lived in groups for a reason, but the old redwood just wanted to be alone, and something told him that some advice from him could greatly enrich their quest.

"It's not far at all. I thought about moving us there when Mina told me about it, but she said it's too open and we might be spotted if someone is in the area," Tiana told him.

"Do you think you could help me get there tomorrow? And then we can leave the day after?" he suggested.

"You want to leave? But you're..."

"I can still navigate. I just need you and Mina to be my eyes, and I can still give advice and guidance too. There is not telling when or if I will get better and if we wait too much longer, we will lose everything."

"I-I'm sorry," Tiana sniffled, fighting back her tears.

Staryn had been waiting for this. He knew her well enough to know that she'd been blaming herself for what happened to him and somehow, he knew that was the root of the darkness growing within her too. He cursed himself for his weakness and self-pity. If it hadn't been for that he may have noticed it before. He could have addressed it before it had gotten this bad. He just prayed that it wasn't too late to reverse it. As it was, she may never be able to heal, given that healing was the lightest of all the disciplines, but really, he had only himself to blame for that. He'd forgotten his duty to her for a time, and that was unacceptable. "Whatever are you sorry for little one?" he asked gently, trying to use his voice to make up for his inability to touch her.

"I...I made the hole too little...I could have done it different...I made you get hurt and now..." her breath started to hitch as she couldn't get anymore words out.

Staryn realized then that not being able to touch her was going to be the most difficult part of this. He was so used to taking her in his arms when she was upset, or running a hand through her hair, or rubbing her back, or any of a dozen other things that all involved him being able to touch her and he was at a loss of how else to comfort her, but he knew he had to try. "It's not your fault, Tiana," he told her firmly but softly.

"Yes it..."

"No. It's not. I should have been paying more attention, both to the hole and to our surroundings before we even ran into the hunters. The hole was plenty big enough if I hadn't sat up like that at the wrong time. That is not your fault. What could you have done differently?" he asked wondering where her mind was going with that.

"You said something about cracking the ground too. I should have done that. It would have been quicker," Tiana told him.

"Why did you decide not to," Staryn asked, not at all accusingly. He knew she must have had her reasons and wanted to hear her talk them out. Even if it was just a simple matter of she was more comfortable with making a vine wall.

"I was afraid they might not be able to stop in time and they could fall in the hole and get hurt or...or killed," she said, but without the same fear or regret that she would normally use in that time of statement and Staryn quickly picked up on it.

"Then it's good you didn't use that way then," Staryn said clearly.

"If I had, then you wouldn't be hurt so bad," she told him.

"Tiana, listen to me very carefully. Please," Staryn told her and paused for a moment before he began to speak. "If there is a way to protect yourself and others without hurting anyone you should always use that way. Even if it's riskier, like this. Yes, I'm hurt, but if you had cracked the ground, knowing what could happen, and someone died, it would have tainted your light for good, and that is never an option, Tia. Please understand that. You cannot fall to the darkness. No matter what," he was getting rather desperate to be understood by the end.

"I...you mean...I'm turning dark?" Tiana asked fearfully.

"Come lay next to me, little one," Staryn told her. Just because he couldn't hold her didn't mean that the body contact couldn't help her. "You are not turning dark. Yes, your light is damaged. There is some darkness in your heart now, but it is nothing that can't be fixed.

You just have to let go of your fear, anger, and guilt. Okay kiddo?"

"Y-you can fix me?" Tiana asked hopefully burying her head in his neck.

He tilted his head towards her, resting it on top of hers. "No, but I can help *you* fix you."

"What do I have to do?" she asked, determinedly. All she could think of were the bad magicians that hurt people and enslaved them and becoming like that was perhaps her greatest fear.

"First, tell me. Have you ever used it? Have you ever felt the bad feelings when you used your magic?"

"I...yeah. A-a few times," she said, eyes widening as she realized what that meant. "I-I had to though. They were...were coming through the wall, and we had to get you away and I was so tired but I had to make something to carry you, and I could hear them and...and..."

"They made you mad and scared, and that gave you the strength to use your powers enough to make something to carry me," Staryn finished, figuring out the rest of the story from there and felt her nod in response. "I understand, kiddo. Really. It happens. And I can tell you haven't used it much since then, but you have been pushing yourself too hard with trying to heal. There's been a little bleedover. You will never be able to heal until the darkness is leeched from your spirit though. And it never will be if you keep pushing yourself so hard."

"But you need..."

"I will be fine, Tia," Staryn told her, pressing a kiss to her head. "I am in no danger of death. You've made me a very comfortable cart. You have to take care of yourself first. Do you remember when we were first learning your powers and you kept trying too hard and couldn't get anything done because of it? It's the same thing here. Except now, when you push yourself too hard, you give the darkness more of you and then you won't be able to heal at all. Ever. So, take care of yourself first, little one. I will be fine until you can help me more. Promise?"

"O-okay. I promise," Tiana said worriedly. "You can tell if the darkness is in me?"

"I can. I'm sorry I wasn't paying enough attention before now to see it," Staryn said guiltily.

"But you'll tell me if it gets stronger or if I'm using it or something right?"

"I will. That is my job after all," he joked, nudging her playfully with his head. "I'm sorry I forgot that for a while," he sobered quickly. Not only did he abandon her this past week to feel sorry for himself, but even before that, he had let down his guard enough for them to nearly be caught and killed in the first place.

"S'okay Staryn," she said earnestly as she cuddled closer to him and kissed his cheek, putting a smile on his face for the first time since this whole mess began.

The next morning, after Tiana fed Staryn and herself, she pulled back the vines from the wheels of the carriage so that it would roll again, and managed with some effort to pull it outside and hook it up to

Mina who would pull them to the clearing. Tiana climbed up next to Staryn and whispered to him about the trees they were passing, the colors of the leaves, the rocks and bushes and anything and everything else she could see. She was taking her task of being his eyes very seriously and he had mentioned during their long talk the previous day how much it helped to hear voices when he couldn't see anything. How it made him feel less alone, so she had no intention of shutting up.

It only took about fifteen minutes to reach the tree and Tiana guided Staryn's hand to the trunk once Mina pulled them up alongside. He closed his eyes for a moment before he disappeared, and Tiana started. She didn't think she would ever get used to seeing that. She decided that she would be on the safe side this time and raised a wall around the center of the clearing. She considered doing the whole clearing, but she remembered what Staryn said about not pushing herself too hard and that would probably qualify. She was sure she could manage about half of it and she did. She was a bit tired after that, but since she wouldn't need to do anything big again for another day and a half she would be fine, and it kept them safe while they were literally unable to run.

"Why have you sought me out, guide of the chosen?" the redwood asked roughly.

"Well, I didn't exactly 'seek you out'," he told him. "We had a bit of a setback and ended up near here, so I thought, since we were close, it couldn't hurt to see what advice you could offer," he said with a shrug, hoping that he wasn't going to be in trouble for intruding on the ancient's solitude.

"Yes, I had felt the concentration of magic nearby and wondered if you would be coming here. When you didn't come for many cycles, I began to reconsider that idea."

"I'm sorry. I was...well..."

"Lost in self-pity because of what you've lost I'd imagine," the redwood said gruffly.

"Yeah. Kinda," he said, embarrassed.

"You young ones are all the same. You see only what you've lost instead of what you stand to gain."

"What could I possibly gain from this?" Staryn asked confused.

"You have already gained greatly," he said impatiently. "Do you not realize how much sharper your hearing is now? Do you not realize how much more clearly you can sense magic? Most importantly though, the shared hardships will bring you and the chosen closer together. Your paths are growing even more tightly entwined."

"What should I do from here?" he asked.

"You must follow your instincts, young one, and let her in. Those are the two most important things you will ever do."

"Thank you, ancient," Staryn told him gratefully. The old tree had given Staryn more than he would probably ever know. The others had given him a reason to keep going but the old redwood had given him a reason to be happy. He sensed the difference in the air as he was laid back on his little cart and almost immediately felt Tiana's hand in his hair as she started talking to him.

"Are you ready to go back now, or do you want to see anything else while we are out?" Tiana asked.

"Well if it's not too far out of the way, why don't we stop by the brook to refill the water jar," Staryn suggested. "I haven't heard the sound of water in far too long."

"Okay. No problem," Tiana cut off her protests about having plenty of water at the second half of his statement. If Staryn wanted to be near the water, then he could be near the water. They ended up spending the rest of the day out there by the brook, Tiana even splashing Staryn a few times as he laughed. Staryn's laughter lifted Tiana's spirits even higher than the Satyr's as the faint darkness in her core began to lose its hold.

They returned to Tiana's makeshift hut near sunset for one last night before they would get moving again. Staryn had told them that the quickest way at this point would be to follow the brook to the main river which they would then follow to the junction. The next morning, with Staryn's prompting, Tiana removed the structure as if it had never been there. She had to admit that not leaving a trail was probably a good thing and she was glad that Staryn was here to think about these things.

Tiana spent most of the time riding on the cart with Staryn, while talking to both him and Mina. Staryn was rather weak still though so he often napped after lunch, during which time Tiana worked on her meditation as she tried to learn to heal. After the first day, when Staryn figured out where they were, he told them that it would take just over two weeks to reach the meeting of the rivers from here, at their current pace, and Tiana swore that she would be able to heal him, at least some, by then. She checked with Staryn multiple times a day to make sure the darkness was going away and not getting stronger, and it didn't take long before Staryn made the connection between his mood and the decrease in the darkness. It seemed the happier he was, the happier she was and the further the darkness was pushed away.

After that he made sure to keep his spirits as high as he could, often teasing and joking with Tiana and Mina. It had started as a mask to fool Tiana, but the more he pretended to be happy, the more he found himself becoming happy as well. Despite his current situation, he was actually happy. Sure, he couldn't see, couldn't feel anything from the neck down, couldn't walk or move, but he was well taken care of. He was loved, and seeing Tiana's happiness reflecting his own made that even more obvious. Before, he had been the caregiver in their relationship, and he still was in many ways. She was still such a little girl. But now, she was taking care of him just as much, and he could see what the old redwood meant when he said that their paths were becoming more entwined. He could see how this was bringing them closer.

It was five days after they had gotten back on the path, when Staryn woke after his nap to Tiana's hands on his head as he felt a tingling going through his skull. He started shifting uncomfortably at the sensation even as he opened his own senses to watch her powers. He knew what she was doing and he suspected that she wouldn't have the power to heal him completely in one shot. Sure enough, it was only a few minutes before he had to say, "Tiana, Stop!"

"I-I'm okay," she said panting a bit.

"No. You're not. You're pushing yourself too hard again. I'm glad that you've managed to find enough healing ability to start helping, but you have to go slowly, Tia, please."

"He is right, little one," Mina told her. "You mustn't drain your powers too much or you may never be able to heal again. He knows your limits better than either of us do. Listen to him."

"Okay. I will," Tiana said breathing deeply as she felt the exhaustion settling over her. "Did I help at all?" she asked as she curled up at Staryn's side, resting her head against his neck.

"I can see now," Staryn whispered to her with a smile, feeling the answering smile on Tiana's face even as her breathing started to even out. Staryn turned to press a kiss to her head as he blinked his eyes and tried to bring them into focus. He may have overstated things just a bit, when he told her he could see. He could see shapes and colors and blurs, but it was something. He could feel her bubble starting to pop as she realized that when she woke up, so he rushed to assure her that it was still better than it was. That she did help and that she could help more soon. It would end up being another three days before he would let her try again, at which point he was able to see the outlines of things and slightly sharper colors. He thought, if he could walk that is, that he would be able to navigate without too much trouble now. At least his sharper hearing and magical sense wasn't diminishing as his eyesight returned. Perhaps it still would, but the longer he could keep it the better. By the time they reached the meeting of the rivers, they had been through two more rounds of healing and Staryn could see almost perfectly again. It was still doing nothing for the rest of his body though, but he assured her it was okay. It might just take time.

Chapter 11: Neri

"Okay. We're here. Now what?" Mina asked curiously as she pulled them to the meeting of the rivers, desperately hoping they wouldn't have to go out there in it. Water powers or not, she didn't think even Tiana could survive it.

"Not sure. I'm guessing this is the point in the prophecies where I have to 'calm the river's rage to free the ancient from his cage', which fits with what the grove showed me, but I have no idea where to start."

"Can you sit me up a little more?" Staryn asked. He hoped if he could get a better look at the problem he might be able to come up with an idea. Tiana waved her hands and tilted the cart at a steeper angle and Staryn studied it for a moment. "I'm guessing you wouldn't be able to hold back the water from one of the sides?"

"Uh-uh. There's way too much," Tiana told him. "And it's way too fast."

"Okay. What about maybe diverting it somehow?" Staryn considered as he continued studying the layout.

"You mean make it go somewhere else?" Tiana asked confusedly, wondering what would happen to the other side of the rivers if she did that.

"Not far. Maybe...I wonder if we could create like a bridge of sorts. Let one river go over top of the other one," he suggested.

"You think that could work?" Tiana asked as she

considered how she would need to do that. She had gotten much better at working with clay and stone, though she still preferred vines when possible. She spent the remainder of the day trying different methods of creating the bridge, but all of them fell apart before they got far and she was getting beyond frustrated.

"It's okay, Tiana. This isn't supposed to be easy. That's why it's a test. We'll figure it out. We'll sleep on it tonight and come back at the problem in the morning, okay?" Staryn assured her.

"What if I can't do it?" she asked in a small voice. She had gotten a lot better about doubting herself, but sometimes that insecurity managed to slip through.

"Of course, you can do it. It might just take a little time to figure out," Staryn told her as if the very idea were beyond silly, and she had to admit that it did help her feel better. The fact that he had so much faith in her that the idea of failure didn't even cross his mind gave her a little more faith in herself. If nothing else, she refused to let Staryn down. She would live up to the faith he had in her if it was the last thing she did. By the time she returned to the river with enough berries for herself and Staryn, Mina had drunk her fill and was off in search of her own dinner while Tiana climbed up on the cart and began to feed both Staryn and herself.

In the end, Staryn was right. Both about her being able to do it, and taking some time to figure it out. She ended up having to start from the far end and decrease the angle by a lot so that it was a gradual enough incline that the pressure of the rushing water wouldn't crumble it before she could keep building. She finally managed to get it going over, but now it was just making a huge mess and it didn't take long before they were all drenched from the spray. "Maybe try putting sides on it?" Staryn suggested as he coughed out another mouthful of water with a laugh. That seemed to do the trick and there was a bridge carrying one of the rivers over the other and they were both perfectly calm.

"Isn't the pretty birdie supposed to be coming out?" Tiana asked worriedly, afraid she had taken too long.

"I thought so," Staryn said, watching the water's surface. It was only another few minutes before the bird shot up out of the water, going about three feet into the air before crashing on the bank.

"Oh no!" Tiana cried out rushing over to it and lifting it up, despite the fact that it was almost half as big as she was. She carried it over to the cart and set it next to Staryn, noticing that it wasn't conscious. "What do I do?" she asked worriedly.

"His magic seems strong and steady. I'd bet he's just exhausted. Maybe just dry him off and let him rest?" Tiana nodded and pulled one of her dry shirts out of her bag and did as Staryn suggested.

It was a few hours later, and Tiana was feeding Staryn dinner when the bird opened his eyes, and she noticed immediately and held out another berry for him and he plucked it quickly out of her fingers and she giggled. She noticed the strange way the bird was staring at her for the rest of the meal, but ignored it. She did find it hard to find time to feed herself while feeding both of them. "You need to eat too, Tiana," Staryn admonished when he realized that she hadn't had a bite in quite a while.

"I will," she promised. "The pretty birdie just woke up after being hurt. He gets to eat first."

That appellation though was enough to stop the bird in his tracks as he sputtered at her for a moment before he found words. "Pretty birdie?" he asked indignantly. "I'll have you know child that I have been around since the dawn of time. I have seen civilizations rise and fall. I have taught rulers and peasants alike. Pretty birdie indeed," he finished with his beak pointed high in the air and his chest puffed up.

Tiana tilted her head at him as she considered his speech. "Okay. But you're still pretty," she finally said matter-of-factly.

The bird snapped his head down to stare at her, but couldn't actually bring himself to argue against that point, so he settled for, "My name is Neri."

"Hi Neri. I'm Tiana. This is Staryn, and that's Mina," Tiana introduced them.

Neri looked around at the group before he said what he'd been considering while he was letter her feed him. "This is all wrong."

"What do you mean?" Tiana asked worriedly.

"You are too young. You are all too young. You shouldn't be here yet. And the guide...what has happened to the guide? This isn't how things were supposed to go."

Staryn could see Tiana starting to get upset and scared that everything was messed up now, so he jumped in to stop the bird before he could go too far. "Regardless, we are here now, and this is the situation we are presented with, so unless you have some way to fix it, there's no point in making an issue of it," he said staring hard at the bird before cutting his eyes over to Tiana who was hugging her knees to her chest and looking rather melancholy.

Neri had seen enough. He'd seen the little chosen patiently feeding not only her guide, but an injured bird as well, putting her own needs second. He'd seen the way she had introduced the unicorn on the same level as herself and her guide. He'd appreciated the way she handled his rant, and may even admit that he might have over-reacted a bit at being called pretty birdie. He was also rather impressed with the guide though. He had been telling the truth when he said that things weren't supposed to be like this. He was supposed to be whole and uninjured, but he seemed to be taking it in stride, and the way he both allowed the chosen to care for him physically while caring for her emotionally at the same time, impressed him in one so young. That was why he hopped up on the young satyr's chest, and pecked him hard, batting his wings to keep Tiana away when she tried to rush at him and tossing a ring of fire around the unicorn when she too tried to interfere, before bending his head and crying three bright pearly tears into the wound he had opened.

When the buffet of wind stopped, Tiana rushed forward in tears, pushing the bird of Staryn and checking for the wound, stopping short when there was nothing there and then she turned back to the bird. "What was that for?!" she asked upset.

"I am a phoenix child. My tears have far stronger healing properties than all the magic in your little body," he said smugly just as Tiana's attention was drawn away by a twitch of Staryn's hand and she gasped.

"Staryn!" she cried. "Your hand..."

"I can feel it again," he said in awe. "I can feel...everything again," he breathed out as he started twitching his toes.

"It may be some time before you are as well as you were. Your muscles will still be weak and need to be built back up, but as long as you put in the effort you will be as good as new in no time," Neri told him.

"Thank you," he said gratefully, tears welling up in his eyes. "Thank you so much." Staryn managed to lift his finger to wipe a falling tear from Tiana's cheek, which of course just prompted more as she threw herself into his arms and Neri flew up into the tree above them. He still had more to tell them, but he would give them their moment. He could use a bit more of a rest before he started his own journey anyway. He had been fighting against the pull of the water for a very long time.

The next morning, he flew down to join them for breakfast, this time bringing his own berries rather than eating theirs, and no sooner than he settled on the edge of the cart, the young chosen turned to him and asked. "What is a phoenix? How did you get under the water? Do you know where I'm supposed to go next?"

"A phoenix is an immortal bird. Every hundred years we are reborn from the ashes of our own flame, but I have been trapped under the water for more than a thousand years. Unable to renew myself in my flames, so I will need to do so very soon. A phoenix is an immortal bird. Neither sides of the wars trusted me though due to my efforts to stop the fighting. They diverted the rivers to create a vortex and trapped me under there smothered by the opposite of my two elements and unable to escape. You see, there are two ways I can travel. By air like any other bird, or in flame, and I could access neither while trapped under the maelstrom of water."

"That's horrible!" Tiana insisted. "How could they do that?"

"They feared me, just as the dark will always fear the light and the light will always fear the dark. None of them realized that both sides need each other. Balance is essential."

"So, I should let myself be part dark?" Tiana asked worriedly, especially after how hard they worked to cleanse the little bit of darkness she'd taken in from her.

"Oh, no, child. You are the light. If you become shrouded in darkness the light will fall for good. Just as the darkness cannot step into the light, you cannot step into the shadows. You just need to understand that you can never destroy the dark. To destroy the dark would be to destroy the light, as it happened a thousand years ago, so it will happen again if you don't heed my warning, only this time, nothing will survive. Remember that child."

"I will," Tiana promised. "Do you know where I'm supposed to go next? Will you be coming with us?"

"Next you will continue along this east river to the ocean. It is a very long journey, and I have my own journey to take. I will check in with you from time to time, but in the meantime, you must learn as much as you can from those your journey brings to your path. Your guide has already taught you a great deal about the power of life, and the unicorn of healing. Your next stop is to learn your power over water, and will take a great deal of time. You may rest the remainder of the day, but you must move on tomorrow," he told them before he flew off, knowing that they would want to take the day to try and help the guide get back on his feet.

Sure enough, as soon as he left, Tiana turned to Staryn. "Do you want to try and get up?" she asked hopefully.

Staryn bit his lip nervously as he moved his leg experimentally. It had been nearly a month since his legs had held his weight. Mina stepped up next to the cart. "You may hold onto me for support," she offered.

"And me," Tiana said holding out her hand to him. She knew that she wouldn't be able to hold as much of his weight as Mina could, but she could position herself better to keep him steady. Staryn took it tentatively and let Tiana pull him to his feet, using his other hand to pull himself up by Mina's mane and then he was on his feet and Tiana was cheering at him and he couldn't help the grin that broke out on his face. He was standing. On his own feet again. He closed his eyes as the full weight of that thought reached him and he started to wobble a bit. "Careful, Staryn," Tiana said as she moved behind him and held him straight.

"Sorry, Tia," he said with a bright smile at her. "Just gonna take a bit to get used to again."

"That's why we're here," Tiana told him happily. "We'll help as much as we can," she assured him, Mina nodding in agreement. Staryn spent the rest of the day alternating between hobbling around the area, sitting up when resting his legs, and napping. Who knew learning to walk again could be so exhausting. Most of all though, he delighted in being able to feed himself again. That had always been the hardest part for the independent satyr to take. Even when he was first born, he had never been half as helpless as he had been the last month.

By the time the suns had set, Staryn could barely keep his eyes open again, and he pulled Tiana tight against his chest, back in their usual position, now that he could move again, but they still slept on the soft, moss covered cart. Mina had assured them that pulling the cart was no hardship for her and she would be glad to continue to do so. They did intend to walk at least part of the day to rebuild their endurance. Tiana hadn't done much more walking than Staryn had this last month, after all, being attached to his side on the cart, but it would be some time before Staryn had the strength for the long treks on his feet.

It was the next morning before Staryn felt the pulsing warmth against his hand and when Tiana woke he asked her, "When did your egg get so warm?"

"What do you mean? It changed?" she asked curiously.

"Hmm. Maybe it was a gradual change, so you didn't notice, but it's definitely a lot warmer than it was the last time I felt it," Staryn told her.

"Is that a bad thing?" she asked concerned.

"I don't think so. I think it might mean it's getting closer to hatching," he told her.

"You think?" she asked, both excited and apprehensive. "What if..." she trailed off.

"What if what?" Staryn prodded.

"What if I can't take care of it?"

"Are you kidding? You did a great job taking care of me when I needed you, and you've got me and Mina to help you. Whatever hatches out of here, we can handle it. Don't worry so much kiddo," Staryn assured her.

"Staryn is right, child," Mina chimed in. "You have the makings of an excellent caregiver. The last weeks have proven that. You will be well."

Tiana hugged them both in turn before offering her shoulder to help Staryn towards the berries. He wanted to do his part to help and he was getting better on his feet, only needing steadying rather than the support of all or most of his weight, so Tiana was more than capable of doing that herself. It took more than twice as long to gather their breakfasts, but no one said anything about it. Once they finished eating, Tiana realized that they would have to cross the southern river and asked aloud, "How do we get across?"

Staryn was glad he had finished his breakfast, otherwise he may have choked as he couldn't help but huff out a laugh. "You built a bridge strong enough to carry a river. Don't you think you could build one to carry us?"

"Oh. Right," Tiana said sheepishly with a bright blush. "I didn't think of that."

Staryn laughed harder and pulled her in for a side hug while ruffling her hair. Tiana was still too happy that he could do that again to find it annoying so she just grinned at him and rolled her eyes before her hands started dancing in the air, building another bridge, this one going over the water and much easier to build except for the fact that it was a very wide river so it took a little while before they were able to head across and begin the next leg of their journey.

Chapter 12: Fugl

They worked with Staryn for a few hours every day, during the day to build his muscles back up and then for a little while after they stopped for the night, before they fell asleep. They usually used that time to teach Tiana more about using life, but this was more important right now. Other teachers would come and go, but Staryn would always be by her side and able to teach her. They would have plenty of time.

It was a few days before Tiana was woken in the night by a wiggling against her stomach and she snapped awake to see the egg starting to shake. "Staryn! Staryn, wake up. I think it's hatching!" she whispered excitedly, and the sleepy satyr pulled himself to sitting as he looked over her shoulder to the shaking egg.

"Yep. I think it is," he said with a yawn. "You remember what we talked about with eggs hatching?"

"How they need to come out themselves and helping them too much can make them weaker later?"

"That's the one," Staryn said with another yawn as he leaned against the side of the little shelter, ready to doze until it was finished. He knew better than to try and go back to sleep for real. Not with Tiana as excited as she was, but he should be able to doze off here and there during the times her attention was on the egg. This would be a rather long process after all. In between the questions and the calls for him to look, he did manage to get a bit more sleep before the suns rose, and after checking the progress one more time, he realized that it was close, but wasn't going to finish by breakfast. "I'll go grab us some breakfast. I'll bring extra for whatever hatches from the egg."

Tiana snapped her head up to look at him before looking back down at the egg that was now filled with cracks and had a small hole pecked out the side. She bit her lip with indecision and looked back up at Staryn. "Will you be okay?" she asked worriedly.

"I'll have Mina go with me just in case," he promised her. "Your place is here right now."

"Okay. Thanks, Staryn," she flashed him a bright smile and he ruffled her hair as he headed out. He managed mostly on his own, only holding onto Mina for support a few times and to get up when he went for the lower berries. He returned with more than twice the berries he usually did, now that they would soon have another mouth to feed, and just hoped that whatever it was ate berries. He slid a large portion of the haul towards her as he ducked under the leaning roof of the shelter and returned to his place next to her. It was a given that they wouldn't be moving until the hatching was complete, and now that its head was fully visible through the widened hole, Staryn had a pretty good idea of what it was and couldn't help the gasp that pulled from him. "What?" Tiana asked. "What is it? Do you know?" She noticed him staring at the egg and the little reptilian head poking out of it.

"A dragon," he said in awe. "They've been extinct as long as magic has."

"Jaren said that his family held onto this egg since before magic died to give to me. I didn't know that dragons took so long to hatch."

"They don't. Dragons hatch within six months usually. My best guess would be that the last magician put the egg into a stasis of sorts until your magic woke it up and started it growing again. This is...incredible." Staryn reached out a hand and touched a finger to the dragon's beak as if to make sure it was real. He got confirmation as he jerked his hand back with a yell and put the bleeding finger in his mouth. Yep. Definitely real. And rather cranky.

"Are you okay!?" Tiana asked worriedly pulling his finger from his mouth and giving it a quick heal, before turning to the baby and saying, "Bad dragon. No biting," while shaking her index finger at it and the dragon let out a little sneeze followed by a puff of flame. Staryn couldn't help but chuckle at that, and Tiana turned back to him. "He's not poisonous or anything is he?"

"Nah. Not yet. He will be when he's fully matured. At least most species of dragon are, but none of them have venom as babies and it's a good thing too since they have a tendency to bite...well...everything."

"What species do you think he is?" Tiana asked curiously, wondering if Staryn would know.

"Well he's obviously a fire species or a hybrid, but that only rules out a few. Once I can see his...there we go. A wing. Definitely a hybrid of some kind. That narrows it down considerably. Unless he is a brand new kind or one that was long extinct even before magic died, there are only a few species of hybrid."

"Like what?" Tiana asked inquisitively.

"Well, most of them are simply recognized by their powers. Hybrids mean that they have access to more than one type of power, so it might be fire and water or fire and air or air and water or water and life. Most have fire as one of their aspects, but not all of them. The only one that is referred to separately is the great dragon or the father dragon depending on who you ask. They can use all of the types of powers and legend says that all other species of dragons were spawned from them," Staryn explained what he knew, suddenly glad that his home grove had been adamant that he learn beings as well.

"I bet this one is a father dragon then," Tiana told him. "I bet the old magician wanted to save the one that could bring the others back too."

"That would make sense," Staryn told her.

"How will we know?" she asked.

"Once he's fully out and cleaned off, I should be able to make a good guess."

It was another hour before the little dragon was fully extricated from the egg and Tiana reached out tentatively to touch him and she felt the tingling going through her hand as her power calmed him enough to allow her to dry him off before she started feeding him the berries. "Are berries good for him or is there something else he should be eating?" she asked.

"Dragons, in their early life, will eat just about anything, but once they reach puberty they only eat meat. Thankfully, by then he will be able to hunt on his own because I can't see either of us actually managing to kill something for him," Staryn said with a shudder. He knew that it was the natural order of things, and some things were predators and some things were prey, but he was most definitely not a predator and the idea of killing something himself made his skin crawl. "If he is a father dragon, which I think he is, he may be a little more open to a broader diet, but it will still primarily involve meat."

"Do you have a name little dragon?" Tiana asked softly. "Can he talk?" she asked Staryn.

"Probably not yet. From what I understand, dragons learn to talk from listening to their caregivers. Dragons in the wild seldom learn, but those in contact with people take a few months to pick it up. You get to name him," Staryn told her.

"Hmm. How about...Fugl," she suggested. "What do you think, little dragon? You like the name Fugl?" He didn't react at all, save to keep plucking the berries from her hand and scarfing them down like he was starving, but he didn't react badly either, so she would take it. "Fugl it is, then," she said as she scratched the top of his head and he laid down bonelessly, but not letting it stop his eating.

Staryn laughed and said, "Maybe you should call him Hungry instead." Tiana giggled along with him, and eventually the dragon finished all the rest of the berries

Staryn had picked. He had eaten as much as both of them put together and he was less than a quarter Tiana's size and both human and Satyr decided they would start picking even more berries from now on. Staryn had heard that dragons ate a lot, but hadn't quite anticipated just how much. Once he was finally finished eating, Staryn said, "We should hit the road. We can still get a few hours in before lunch."

"Yeah okay. Come on Fugl," she said despite not giving him a choice as she bent down and picked him up, carrying him to the cart where she and Staryn both climbed up and were soon deeply asleep after being up nearly the entire night with the hatching egg. Thankfully for them, Fugl seemed content to sleep as well after his big meal and took the same place his egg had for the last months, curled into a little ball at Tiana's stomach.

When they stopped for lunch, Fugl toddled along behind them to the berry bushes and scarfed up every berry that had already fallen to the ground while Staryn and Tiana pulled the ripe berries that were still attached to the bush, heading back to the cart and Mina to eat, as was habit. They quickly realized they were going to have to change that habit though. Despite eating enough for about five people, Fugl was still begging their berries. "Maybe we should start eating while we pick like he does," Staryn suggested.

Tiana nodded, wondering for a moment why they hadn't done that all along and then she remembered that she used to have bread. Staryn would go get her berries and bring them back for her to eat with her bread. That though sent a pang of longing through her at all the things she was missing. Bread, jam, milk, sugar, even meat. She could barely remember what they tasted like anymore. And the people. She couldn't remember what any of the townspeople looked like. Not Ms. Jilly with the horses. Not Mr. Noct who ran the general store. The only one she could really remember was the woman with the baby, and she didn't even know her name. Their dying moments would be etched into her mind forever. Even her father's face and voice were starting to fade from her memory and she could feel the moisture on her cheeks as the tears fell.

"What's wrong?" Staryn asked worriedly as he reached out to wipe away the tears.

"I...I can barely remember what my father looks like anymore," she sniffled.

Staryn wasn't sure what brought that up, but he decided that it didn't matter. He didn't really understand the attraction of parents having been raised by the forest as a whole and seeing them all as his parents in a way, but he knew from their long talks at the beginning that for her it was something special and important. He wasn't even sure if it was a human thing or if it was unique to her, but it didn't matter. She was upset, and he would find a way to fix it. "Wait here," he told her, winding his way into the woods.

It wasn't until he was out of sight that she realized that he had just gone off on his own when he could still barely walk. Before she could get too worked up over the idea though, he came back into view holding something behind his back, not pulling it out until he had plopped back down on the cart and they were moving again. He pulled the large piece of tree bark, about two feet square out from behind his back along with a stick and a sharp rock. "I know you said you liked to draw, so I thought maybe you could use the rock to draw him on here, and then when you're done we can use juice from the berries and color from the dirt or whatever else we need to color it and then we can carry it around with us so you never have to worry about forgetting."

Tiana launched herself into his arms, tears falling fast and free on his shoulder as he rubbed her back soothingly. "Thank you," she whispered gratefully. She should have known Staryn would find a way to make her feel better. He always did. Even when she thought it wasn't possible. Once she had pulled herself together she settled in Staryn's lap, leaning back against him as she began carving with the rock. She tried tying it to the stick first, figuring that was Staryn's intention, but found that it worked much better with the rock held tightly between her fingers.

She continued to work at the carving for the rest of the day, but Staryn pulled her out of it for dinner. He told her it wasn't good for her to bury herself in it. She had to remember that the rest of the world was out here too. At least he had her responsibility to the little dragon to hold over her as well. They ended up getting a decent routine going, during which Staryn would take care of Fugl in the afternoons so she could work on her carving, if she would be present with them the rest of the time.

It was two days in before she noticed the tingling in her hand as she was carving and looked closer at what she was doing before she sucked in a sharp breath. She wasn't quite halfway done, but it looked so much like him. She could even see the laugh lines by his eyes. It was almost like it could come alive at any moment. She knew that she wasn't near that good at drawing, even on level paper with real writing implements. Her magic must be helping her along. Helping her transfer what's in her mind onto the bark. Now she understood more why Staryn would only let her work for a while each day. He wouldn't want her to drain her powers too much.

It took her five days to put the finishing touches on the carving and the next day she started with the color. She saved some of the berries from her breakfast and used the lighter red ones to stain his lips and the dark ones for the little things like the center of his eyes and his nostrils and such. She gathered clay from their path over the course of the day to color his skin, but it was a few days before they managed to find something that could be used to make white paints for his hair, teeth, and the rest of his eyes and then it was finally finished.

It was finished just in time too, because Fugl was really getting to be a handful and he didn't listen to Staryn nearly as well as he did to Tiana. Not that he didn't like Staryn, of course. He did see the satyr as an authority figure. Just not as much as Tiana. It helped

that Tiana's powers instinctively calmed him. Tiana
came up with the idea of letting him trot behind them
rather than riding on the cart. She said maybe he was
getting restless and now that he was the size of a small
goat, he was moving fast enough to keep up.

It was a few days later when they realized what at
least part of Fugl's issue was. They were foraging for
berries when suddenly he stopped and turned away
from them, crouching down, and tilting his head to the
side while putting his nose in the air, as if listening and
smelling at the same time. Just before Tiana was about
to ask him what he was doing, he pounced. He still
wasn't flying yet, but for short hops he could get
enough air beneath his wings to carry him a little farther
and a moment later he trotted back to them carrying a
squirrel in his mouth and plopped down to the ground
to start tearing into it.

Staryn swallowed audibly, willing the bile back
down as he turned away, looking a little pale. He had
known that the sight wouldn't really sit well with him,
given his deep connection with all the plants and
creatures of the forest, but he hadn't quite expected it
to hit him that hard. Maybe he could talk the dragon
into eating those sorts of things somewhere else.

Tiana, while also slightly disgusted by the sight,
was partially wondering how she could get Fugl to catch
her some meat too. It had been a long time since she'd
eaten anything but nuts and berries. She was worried
how Staryn would take it though. She knew that he
didn't eat meat at all, and judging by the look on his

face now, and the way he was avoiding looking at Fugl, it probably wouldn't sit well with him, so she put the idea out of her mind. At least for a while.

After eating the squirrel, Fugl seemed much easier to handle, and they quickly figured out that he was reaching the age that he needed to eat more meat and he had been getting cranky from not having any. From that point on, when Tiana and Staryn went for berries, Fugl went hunting. He never went far from them though. It wasn't until nearly a week later when he brought down a large rabbit, and then a belch of fire cooked it up nice, that Tiana's craving for meat hit her again along with the smell and she watched Fugl tear the cooked rabbit apart with a hunger in her eyes. She didn't even notice Staryn's eyes on her until he asked, nose crinkled in distaste, "That makes you hungry?"

Tiana started and turned to look at him, biting her lip worriedly. "I'm sorry. I know you don't like that. It's just...it's been so long since I've eaten meat and..."

"You eat meat?" he asked curiously, his face softening. He hadn't realized that. He'd assumed that since they were so similar physiologically and she had never said anything, that she had mostly the same diet as he did. "Why didn't you ever say? We might have been able to figure something out." He didn't think that he would ever have been able to kill an animal, even to feed her, but he could have at least asked the trees to keep an eye out for animals that were already dead.

"You were being so nice keeping me fed, and I knew you didn't eat meat and you loved all the animals so much, I didn't want you to be mad at me," she said nervously, looking down at the ground, too scared to see the disgust on his face.

The next thing Tiana knew there was a gentle hand under her chin and she felt her face being turned up. "I could never be mad at you. I understand that different beings have different dietary requirements. I'm not mad a Fugl for eating meat. Nor have I ever been mad at a cougar or a wolf for doing the same. If you eat meat, we will get you meat. I do have to admit, I'm a little glad we can send Fugl out to do the hunting now," he ended with a joke, giving her nose a tweak. "It's my job to take care of you, kiddo. You have to tell me if you need something," he added sternly seeing her nod.

Chapter 13: Running Away

Tiana managed to talk Fugl into catching her an extra critter for dinner every few days as she chewed over another idea of something that she needed, but was also hesitant to bring up to Staryn for obvious reasons, but nearly two weeks later, she still couldn't get the idea out of her head, so she bit the bullet. "You know how you said if I needed anything I should let you know?" Tiana asked worrying her lower lip between her teeth.

"Of course," Staryn said giving her his full attention. "What do you need?"

"I...um...I need to find a village to sneak into. I really need some real clothes and want to get more bread and maybe even some other foods that I miss," she told him.

"No. Uh-uh. No way. There has to be another way," Staryn said shaking his head emphatically.

"Do you know how to sew clothes? Because I know I don't," Tiana pointed out.

"What's wrong with what you're wearing?" he asked, still not understanding exactly why she needed clothes in the first place, but accepting it as a human thing.

"Well for one, these aren't even supposed to be dresses. They are Jaren's old shirts and he just gave me the rope to tie them up. Besides there's hardly anything left to them anymore. There's more hole than shirt."

"And that makes it okay to sneak into a human village...alone since you know neither Mina nor I could go with you. Are you crazy?!" he asked incredulously.

"You said if I needed something you'd make sure I got it. You said it was your job! And I need something to wear that isn't falling apart," she snapped petulantly before storming off into the woods in irritation. She had heard too many people call her papa crazy to like hearing that word and to hear Staryn of all people call her that, really hurt.

"Tiana! Wait!" Staryn called out as he started to rush after her, but Mina stopped him.

"Perhaps it would be better to let me," she suggested and Staryn sagged as if his strings had been cut and nodded, reaching over to unhook the cart so that she could have better maneuverability in the thicker trees that Tiana had darted into. As Mina headed into the foliage, Staryn collapsed onto the cart and put his head in his hands. How could he have been so stupid? He could tell that she was nervous about asking him to begin with and then he goes and flies off the handle about it. No wonder she ran off. It went against every instinct he had not to go after her himself, but he knew that in this case, Mina was right. She probably wouldn't want to see him anytime soon, anyway.

It didn't take Mina long to catch up to Tiana, the pull of the young chosen still strong, leading directly to her. "You probably shouldn't get too far away," Mina told her.

"The trees told me there is a village not far from here," Tiana told her, stomping through the forest on her way.

"I thought you couldn't understand the trees," Mina said, trying to think of some way to stop this foolishness without getting Tiana angry at her too.

"I asked where the nearest village was, and they started leading me. If there wasn't one nearby they wouldn't have done anything," she told the unicorn. She could understand that much.

"Tiana wait. You really shouldn't..."

"Oh, you think I'm crazy too?" she snapped at the unicorn.

"No. You're not crazy. Just...maybe we should talk about this a little more first. You remember what happened last time we ran across humans."

"That was a long time ago and a long way from here. Who says word about me has even travelled this far? And even if it has, that word probably says I'm travelling with you and Staryn, so they probably wouldn't even recognize me on my own."

"That sounds like a lot of hoping and probablys," Mina said nervously. "You know Staryn is just concerned for your safety. He was speaking out of fear."

"It's not like I'm a baby anymore. I can protect myself just fine if I need to," she snapped irritated, and Mina realized that the little girl wasn't going to hear a thing she said. She followed Tiana in silence to the treeline at the edge of the village before turning around and running as fast as she could back to Staryn now that she knew where it was.

The unicorn burst out of the trees by the cart and said, "Tiana's in the village."

"She's WHAT!?" Staryn yelled jumping to his feet. He should have kept his mouth shut. He should have discussed all this calmly and tried harder to find another way or talk her out of it or something. Now she was going to die, and it was all his fault. "You know where?" he asked the unicorn and when she nodded, he jumped on her back and said, "Take me there."

Mina took no offense at his tone, given the situation and did as he asked with as much speed as she could manage, right up until the weight on her back disappeared. "Staryn?" she released into the ether, unable to find his mind at the moment, and she started to panic as she tried to figure out what had happened to him. After a moment she remembered that when he had gone into the trees before, she hadn't been able to sense his mind then either and there were plenty of trees around that could have grabbed him. She really wished the timing was better though or that she knew what to do. Standing here waiting while Tiana could be in trouble wasn't the best idea, but getting Staryn to her if she did get in trouble would be. If only she knew how long he would be. She paced the area for a few minutes before she huffed and shook her head, taking off to the edge of the village to wait and watch as much as she could. If Tiana needed a quick getaway, she may be the only option.

Staryn could feel the trees whipping past him as Mina ran, but it was as he felt his leg brush past one of them when the wind was suddenly gone, and he felt himself surrounded by a familiar warmth. If it had been any other time, he probably would have relaxed into it, but he didn't have time for this now. He started to struggle against it, but he felt the hold on him tighten and he couldn't get away. "Will you stop and listen already?" he heard a stern voice say and he sagged and stopped struggling, now that he knew it wouldn't do any good.

"Tiana. She's in trouble..."

"The chosen is well, young guide," the tree assured him.

"She's in the village and the people...they..."

"We are aware. We led her there, and word has travelled of your previous confrontation," the tree told him.

"Then how could you..." Staryn started indignantly.

"Because she must learn to stand on her own feet. And you must learn to let her. You are to be her guide, not her warden, young one."

"But she's so little. And it's so dangerous," Staryn protested fearfully.

"She is. And it is. You have been teaching her though. Do you not think that she could extricate herself from the danger? Do you not think that she could save herself if the need arises?" the tree asked, making it very clear who he thought was at fault if she couldn't.

"I don't know," Staryn admitted ashamedly. "If she's thinking straight then she could, yes, but she tends to panic."

"And as long as you are by her side, holding her hand, she will always feel free to panic because she will know that you will save her."

"But she's so young. She's still just a baby," Staryn pointed out. "She shouldn't have to…"

"Regardless of should or should not, she does have to. She is too young for this job, yes. So are you. Nevertheless, it is on her shoulders, and yours. There is no longer the luxury of those excuses." Staryn tried to straighten himself up and look brave and strong even as he fought back his tears. They were right. No more excuses. The forest saw that the tough love had done its job and softened greatly with their next words. "You wish to care for her and protect her, young Staryn, and that is admirable. You must also learn to let her fly as well though. It is for you to push her forward, not hold her back."

"I…I know. I guess…I just forgot that for a while. I'm sorry," he said sadly and waited until he felt the forgiving embrace before he asked, "Will you send me to where you sent her?"

"What do you intend to do?" he was asked with a hint of warning in the tone.

"Observe, and be there if she gets in too much trouble," Staryn said quickly.

"As long as you remember that if you are spotted,

she will be in far more danger than she is now."

"I know. Mostly, I just want to be there when she gets back. To apologize and make things right between us again."

"Then I will send you," the tree replied before Staryn felt the squeezing sensation that marked travelling through the trees. It was a rather unique sensation, that Staryn was long used to, but no one else could manage. Perhaps Tiana with her talent with life could handle it, but it would likely still be quite uncomfortable. Staryn though was part of the trees. He had come from them. Their ways were a comfort to him. He arrived near the edge of the woodline, and crouched behind the nearest large tree as his eyes scanned what he could of the village before they finally lit on a tiny shape darting through the shadows. He could feel his heart in his throat as he struggled to breathe through his fear, but kept himself from interfering. He knew that the trees were right. His interference would just cause much more danger for her.

He had been watching for a few minutes when he heard hoofbeats, and quickly melded into the tree until he realized it was Mina, and he stepped back out. "Oh, it's just you," he said with relief as he turned back to the village, finding Tiana again.

"How long have you been here and how did you get here so quickly?" Mina asked slightly annoyed.

"Not for too long. The trees sent me. After knocking some sense into me."

"They sent you?" she asked curiously, despite her eyes following the same small dot his were. He gave her a brief overview of the travel, along with how fast it was, and how it had saved Tiana's life when they had first met. "So, this is a human village?" Mina asked, trying to pass the time and keep her mind off of what was going on out there.

"I suppose. This is the first I've seen as well," he told her with a shrug. "There sure are a lot of them though."

"That is an understatement," Mina agreed. She could not have imagined so many humans in one place. In fact, she wasn't sure she would have imagined so many humans in the world. There must have been hundreds of them out there.

Tiana slipped into the shadows behind the outermost house and crept around slowly. She was looking for something in particular, but if she couldn't find it she would take what she could get. As she darted from one house to the next, she finally found what she was looking for at the fourth house as some children's clothes were hanging on the line. There were even a bunch of dresses that looked to be her size. She didn't want to take everything this little girl had though, so she was just going to grab two of them before she stopped short. This was stealing. Stealing was wrong.

She chewed her lip for a moment as she considered her options. Stealing was wrong, but trade was good. She knew how that worked and her father had always traded things for other things. She grinned and held out her hands, twitching her fingers around as she weaved a group of vines into a beautiful little doll and then grabbed the two dresses off the line and hung the doll in their place.

She ducked into a nearby barn to change into one of the dresses and noticed a large jug of fresh milk sitting off to the side and she considered what she could trade for the milk before she noticed that the goat was lame. Its leg was twisted around, and it probably would have been put down long ago if the farmer hadn't needed it for milk. She stepped over to the goat and put her hands over the leg and sent a burst of healing to it. It didn't take much, fortunately. The bone had a clean break. It was far easier to heal than Staryn had been. That done, she took the jar of milk and set off looking for a bakery cart, already considering what she could trade for some bread and possibly even a pie if she got lucky.

It took her a little while to find one without being spotted and she darted around back of the nearest building, making sure that no one was around before she started pulling vines into nice baskets. She knew that bakers always needed baskets to put their breads in, so it would be a fair trade. She made five of the baskets before she ducked her head around the corner to watch for an opening. She waited until the baker rushed away from his cart to help an old lady who dropped her bags before she darted forward, dropped the baskets behind the cart and shoved four loaves of bread into her bag along with the dress and the jug of milk and she grabbed a pie as she darted back around the corner to let the adrenaline loose before she started making her way towards the trees.

She knew Mina was probably still waiting for her, but she just wanted to get to the woods first, then she would circle back around to where she had left the unicorn. She hadn't anticipated both Mina and Staryn watching her like a hawk and circling around to her first. No sooner than she stepped past the first group of trees, she was pulled into a tight hug, barely managing to save the pie from falling before shuffling forward, pulling Staryn with her, enough to set it on Mina's back for the moment and then she was hugging Staryn too.

"I'm sorry, Tia. I'm so sorry," Staryn babbled. "I should have listened to you. We should have talked about it. Just please, please promise me that you'll never run off like that on your own again. I'll try to be more accepting about letting you go, but at least let me help you plan and be waiting in case you need me, okay?"

"Okay, Staryn. I promise. I just had to this time," she told him, feeling a little guilty herself about running off like that.

"I know, but we can talk later. For now, let's get out of here before those people realize that anything is going on," Staryn told her and for the first time in a while, Mina had two passengers as they headed back to where they had left the cart.

Little did they know, but when the people realized

what had happened, they decided to write it off as a rash of good luck. Not all villages were as closed minded as the ones near Tiana's home. They had heard of the little witch and the demon, and the townspeople were of two different minds about the matter. Those who believed it but thought that getting on their bad side would be the height of folly, and those who thought that the story had been exaggerated to persecute a little girl who may or may not have powers. The three people who were touched by Tiana that day were of the second group as the mother went to retrieve her washing to find herself missing two dresses, but marveling at the beauty of the doll that was left in their place. She got a bright smile as she took the doll in to her daughter. It was worth far more than two dresses, after all.

The farmer went to retrieve the jug of milk just after Tiana had slipped out and stopped short when it wasn't there. As he looked around though he realized that the lame goat was walking again, and he felt his heart leap for joy. His prayers had been answered. He hadn't been able to afford a new goat and with this one unable to pull a cart or even walk, he had been having a difficult time for a long time. It wasn't until the initial euphoria passed that he wondered how it was possible and remembered the missing milk as well as the stories of the little witch and he grinned and said aloud in case she was still nearby. "Thank you, little witch. You're welcome to return for more milk anytime you need." For this he would share his milk with her for the rest of his life.

The baker returned to his cart and stopped short before looking around quickly. There were definitely things missing from the cart, but it wasn't until he walked around the back that he noticed the stack of baskets and picked them up, marveling at the craftsmanship and detail. These were the finest baskets he had ever seen, and he quickly decided that these would not be for trade. They would be for his personal use. It wasn't until he heard the farmer's story that he and the mother managed to put two and two together and realize that the little witch had been shopping in their town. Like the others, he held no ill will towards her though. Just one of those baskets was worth everything she took and the three of them all considered themselves blessed.

Chapter 14: Amitiel

Once they got back to the cart, they started moving again, still following the great river towards the sea as Staryn and Tiana talked things out. He admitted that he may have overreacted a bit about the idea and she admitted that running off on her own without a plan may have been a little reckless and they managed to find a nice middle ground for the next time she felt like she needed to do something risky. Partway through the conversation, Tiana pulled over the pie and stuck her fingers in, pulling out a large bite and putting it in her mouth, offering it to the Satyr to try. After his first try at bread, Staryn was more than a little skeptical about this potential perversion of his beloved berries, but at the hopeful look on her face, he decided to give it a shot. He reached in and pulled out a small taste of the gloop and visibly steeled himself before placing it in his mouth. It didn't take long for his eyes to widen and he reached for more causing Tiana to laugh.

A few more bites and he sat back, and Tiana tilted her head curiously at him. "You don't want anymore?"

"No, it's okay. You were the one who got it. You should get to eat most of it," Staryn told her.

"I got it for both of us. I got lots of bread that neither of you will eat, and I know Mina isn't a fan of berries, so she probably won't like the pie either, so the least you can do is eat the one thing I can share," she said with a huff. "It's not like you've ever let me refuse to eat something that you went and got us."

Staryn blinked at her for a minute before he realized that she may actually be offended by his refusal to share her food and he tried to put himself in her shoes. If he had went and braved danger to get something to share with her and then she refused it, he supposed he would be hurt. They'd always shared everything before, except for the fruits she'd brought back from the grove and even then, she had tried to share. This was much like that had been, in that it was something that she loved, and it was finite, but the cat was already out of the bag on that one. She already knew he liked it, and he just couldn't bring himself to hurt her feelings anymore, so he reached back for it. "Okay, I'll have some more. I just know this is all we have and since I like the regular berries just fine, I wanted to save more of this for you is all." There. Now she understood his reasoning and had the option to take him up on it. Not that he expected her to, of course.

"And I've had lots of pies before. This is your first. All the reason for you to have more," she argued. Staryn just shrugged at that and continued to eat tilting his head curiously at Tiana as she pulled the jar of milk out of the bag and drank a good portion of it down. She handed it over and he took a tentative sip before spitting it back out and she laughed brightly. "I take it you don't like milk."

"That is milk? I thought it was only for infants not

yet weaned?" Mina asked curiously.

"I think in lots of animals it is, but in humans even old people drink milk," Tiana told her. "I don't know why."

"Huh. Strange," Staryn said thoughtfully.

"Yeah, I guess it is strange," Tiana said tilting her head thoughtfully as she wondered why that was. It didn't stop her from turning back the jar again though. She knew that it would only be good for another day or two and since she was apparently the only one who would drink it, she would need to be quick about it. She hadn't even considered offering some to Fugl until he hopped on the edge of the cart and started sniffing at the jar. "Oh, I'm sorry Fugl. Did you want to try some?" she offered, tilting it towards him, but once he got a good sniff he huffed and hopped back off the cart, resuming running behind them as he usually did in the afternoons.

Fugl had settled into a good rhythm with them as well. He did most of his hunting after they had all gone to bed, settling down to sleep himself in the early hours of the morning and he usually slept until lunch before running and gliding after the cart in the afternoons. He was managing to get more and more lift during his jumps and Tiana wondered how much longer it would be before he was actually flying. He was getting better at talking to them. He still couldn't use words or anything, but he could get simple concepts across by sending images to their minds. Thankfully, he seemed to understand everything they said at least.

By the time two more weeks had passed, Fugl was bigger than Mina and was now regularly bringing down horses and deer, of which he would separate a decent sized chunk for Tiana each evening. Mina could no longer pull him on the cart, so he ended up sleeping at night and hunting in the morning now that he was getting better at flying short distances, he could fly overhead and scan the area so as not to lose them when they were on the move. The biggest problem they had was the fact that Fugl was so used to curling up with Tiana and Staryn to sleep, but he took up the whole cart now. Expanding the cart would be problematic when it came to maneuvering through the trees. As it was they had to regularly go around any thicker vegetation that Tiana couldn't move temporarily. Eventually they compromised by having Fugl sleep next to the cart and just rest his head up with them.

When Tiana asked, Staryn told her that Fugl would end up being far larger than he was now. There was a reason that dragons like him usually lived in the mountains or in the sea. Getting around anywhere else tended to be a nightmare. By the time they reached the ocean a few weeks later, he was already having trouble getting around the trees and spent most of his time in the air above them just to make things easier. Now that there was an open beach however, Fugl came in for a hard landing, kicking sand up in every direction as Tiana, Staryn, and Mina all groaned as they tried fruitlessly to brush themselves off.

They were so distracted by the sticky irritating sand covering their skin that they didn't even notice their visitor for a while. Eventually, Staryn noticed the movement out of the corner of his eye and elbowed Tiana, jerking his head towards her. Tiana looked over and her eyes widened as she stepped forward to introduce herself, Staryn at her back as always. "Hello. I am Tiana," she said trying not to betray her nerves.

"I am Amitiel," came a high-pitched, almost painful sounding voice as the girl flapped her tail. She looked to be slightly older than Tiana, and had long flowing dark indigo hair and eyes to match. Her skin also took on a rather bluish hue, more of an arctic blue/white that didn't seem particularly out of place. Her tail was the same darker blue as her hair and eyes. "You come learn," Amitiel questioned motioning out to sea, clearly uncomfortable with the language.

"I...I don't know how to swim," Tiana said nervously, realizing that as a water element that was possibly unforgivable, but she'd never had occasion to learn. There was no large body of water near her village and the river they had been following for the last couple months was too fast to really learn in.

"You come learn," Amitiel said more clearly holding out her hand to Tiana. "Water not hurt chosen." Tiana took a deep breath for courage before reaching out to Amitiel's hand, clutching Staryn's in her other one. Amitiel looked at their joined hands and pulled her own back. "Only chosen come."

Tiana's breathing started to speed up as she began

to lose the battle with calm. She turned towards Staryn and latched onto his side, and he held her nearly as tightly as he closed his eyes and forced him to remember what the trees had told him. He had to learn to let her fly...or swim in this case. He had to push her forward instead of hold her back. He just didn't know if he could. He took a few shaky breaths of his own before he looked directly into Amitiel's indigo eyes. "How long will she be gone?" Staryn asked steadily, ignoring the look of betrayal Tiana shot him.

"Four storms," Amitiel told him.

Staryn had to force himself not to tighten his grip on her at that. That was two years. She would be gone for two years. How could he let her go for that long? How would she cope without him for that long? "Will she be able to come back to visit?" he asked hopefully.

Amitiel seemed to consider the matter for a moment, looking carefully at the little girl clinging to the young satyr for dear life, before she nodded. "After each storm end," she agreed.

"I don't want to go, Staryn," Tiana lost the battle with her tears as she clung to him tighter and he swallowed around the lump in his throat as he extricated himself from her grip, and knelt in front of her.

"I know you don't, little Tia. I don't want you to go either, but Amitiel has a lot to teach you. This is one part of your journey that I can't come with you on, but you know I won't be far," he promised.

"Why can't you come?" she sniffled.

"Because I am a being of life. Not of water. It can't hurt you, but it would hurt me," Staryn said gently.

"I don't want to leave you," she said weakly, knowing that she didn't have a choice. "I don't want to be alone again," she added almost inaudibly.

"And I don't want you to leave either, kiddo, but it has to be done. I'll be standing right here waiting every time you get to come visit and when you're done. I promise," he vowed as he pressed a kiss to her forehead, wiping her tears with his thumbs. "And you won't be alone. I bet you and Amitiel will be best friends in no time, and in fact, hang on," he looked around her to Amitiel and said, "Her dragon friend is a water-hybrid. Will he be able to come with her?"

"Water come," Amitiel said with a nod.

Staryn nodded gratefully as he turned his attention back to Tiana. "And Fugl will be with you too. I will miss you dearly, little one, but you will be back before you know it," he put on a brave face despite wanting nothing more than to fall apart.

Tiana gave another plaintive sniffle, but she nodded before throwing her arms around Staryn's neck and hugging him tightly. "I'll miss you so much, Staryn. I promise I'll learn as quick as I can so I can come back."

"Just remember not to push yourself too hard," he warned giving her one more tight squeeze before letting her go.

"I won't," she told him before going over to Mina, to say her goodbyes there too. "I'll miss you too, Mina," she said sadly reaching up to wrap her arms around the unicorn's neck as it lowered to her level and Mina's head wrapped around her lovingly.

"I will miss you as well, child. As your guide said, we will be here waiting each time you return," she too promised.

While Tiana was saying her goodbyes to Mina, Staryn walked over to Fugl and reached up to scratch the top of his head the way he liked. "You'll take good care of her right?" he asked worriedly, having to redouble his efforts to keep his tears at bay. He just had to hold on a little longer until she was safely away. He received an image of Tiana curled up against his stomach protectively and realized that it was Fugl's promise to care for her. It was followed by an image of a storm that held a hint of a question. "You want to know what we'll do for the storms?" Staryn asked and Fugl nodded, having long picked up that mannerism. "I'm not sure. We haven't really thought that far ahead yet," he admitted, knowing that it was an oversight. There were only two more weeks before the storm season would start, but he had been so intent on getting Tiana here that he hadn't considered what would come next. Fugl apparently had though. He looked up towards the hills that were likely just a day's walk near the way they had come and sent Staryn an image of a system of caves and himself hunting in them the last couple days and clearing them out. "You think we should go there?" Fugl nodded again and Staryn thanked him. He noticed Tiana finishing with Mina and left Fugl with one more admonishment to take good care of her before pulling Tiana into one more quick tight hug and giving her a little push towards the waiting mermaid.

As Amitiel reached an arm around her, Tiana looked back longingly, one last time, before they disappeared into the ocean with a splash, Fugl jumping right after her, and Staryn finally let the tears fall from his cheeks as he sat heavily in the sand, unable to hold his own weight up any longer. He had no idea what to do with himself without her. She had been his entire reason for being since the moment he was born, and that had only become stronger once they began their journey. How would he get by without her exuberant joy and her boundless energy? How silent would it be without her ringing laughter and the delightful sounds that she always made with her voice that she called music?

He watched the ocean waves for a long while before he pulled himself back to his feet and started walking back the way they came, placing a comforting hand on Mina's back as he did so. The tears were still streaming down his cheeks and neither of them had any words. After walking in a melancholic silence for a few minutes Staryn stopped. "I'm gonna..." he croaked out, gesturing to the large tree next to him and Mina nodded, wishing she had an escape like that of her own, before she realized that she did. Running had always given her a feeling of freedom and exhilaration. When Staryn disappeared into the tree, she turned back towards the beach and the long open space it offered.

As Staryn felt the embrace of the forest wrap around him, he hugged his knees to his chest and cried, finally feeling like he had some idea what Tiana meant when she talked about parents comforting their children. It was a long time, and he was finally feeling under control again, when he heard the low rumbling voice, "We are very proud of you, young Staryn." That was enough to get the tears flowing again, but not quite as miserably. "This separation will be good for both of you."

"How?" Staryn asked plaintively.

"You still have much to learn, little guide. Your journey began too soon. You must learn so that you can teach the chosen. When she returns you will both be ready." Staryn nodded. It would definitely help him pass the time. He was sure it was understood that he would need time off when Tiana was visiting, and that he would take some time with Mina as well, so he wouldn't be in constant study as he had in his formative years, but he knew that the forest was a hard taskmaster and he would be spending more time doing so than he liked.

It was nearly a full day before he pulled himself from the tree's embrace and stepped back out into the forest. They told him where he could find Mina and he headed back towards the beach to find her looking out over the water. "We should rest for the night," he told her, and she nodded and followed him back into the trees. Without Tiana to make a shelter, they would both be in the open, but they would still have the trees to

care for them as they had before she had come into
their lives. They would make way for the caves in the
morning and would use that as their base until Tiana
returned for good.

Chapter 15: The Ocean

Tiana felt an arm around her side and then she was diving through the air and pulled underwater and she could feel herself panicking as the arm gripping her just held her even tighter while she kicked and struggled, trying to hold her breath. It seemed like forever before she couldn't possibly hold her breath one more second and opened her mouth gulping in what she expected to be a lungful of water, but ended up being air. She snapped her eyes open and waited for them to adjust as she took to getting air back in her lungs and tried to figure out exactly what had happened. She took another breath, slower this time, trying to pay attention to exactly what was happening with the water and she realized that the water was stopping just before her mouth and only allowing air through. She could feel the low thrumming in her body that told her that it was something she was causing instinctually, and she realized what Amitiel had meant when she'd said that the water wouldn't hurt her.

About this time, she also realized why Amitiel had trouble with spoken language. Water had its own language too, and it was so much different than anything she had ever experienced before. She wouldn't even know how to describe it. In a way it was like communicating with pure waves of emotion or intent, but it was also so much more than that. For example, she could feel apprehension and remorse from Amitiel who was now floating a few feet away from Tiana and the young chosen considered for a moment and decided to give this strange language a shot and focused on her feelings of betrayal and enquiry. What she received back was too fast and disjointed for her to figure out and after a few moments, Amitiel seemed to realize that so she did the equivalent of slowing down and using simple words. Tiana managed to piece together that the best way to learn was to live it, otherwise she would have always been tempted to panic. She considered that argument and tried to picture herself ever believing that she could do this and realized that Amitiel was right. She would never have been able to do it without being forced. She sent the impression of forgiveness at the mermaid.

That argument settled, she turned to look at Fugl and couldn't help but laugh. It seemed she wasn't the only one who would need to learn to swim. He was so used to flying through the air that he was trying to use his wings the same way. As a hybrid, his wings would work for either environment, but they required different motions to swim than to fly. He was essentially just bobbing in place as he pulled his wings down and his body went up and then pulled his wings up bringing his body down. Now that she was paying attention she could feel the frustration coming from him and Amitiel's amusement joined her own. The mermaid, at least, could do something about it. She swam over to the struggling dragon and pulled the water tighter around her arms so that she seemed to have something much like his wings and showed him how to shift them to draw them back and then flatten them to bring them back forward, spreading them again to draw back. It took a few minutes but soon enough Fugl was cutting through the water at near super speeds and took to making large circles around the girl and the mermaid still sitting there.

Tiana, unfortunately, wasn't so easy to teach to swim. She didn't have wings or flippers or even webbed fingers or toes. Even at her best she would always be terribly slow. She could feel the comfort and acceptance coming from Amitiel though. She thought that the mermaid was trying to tell her that it was okay. That she wasn't expected to be as fast as those who were built to live down here. It didn't much help her feel better though. The idea of Amitiel and Fugl constantly having to hold themselves back for her to keep up didn't sit well with her. Amitiel just smirked at that thought and grabbed Tiana to her chest and began flapping her tail through the water, moving barely slower than her normal pace before motioning to Fugl to do the same. The dragon used his forelegs to wrap around Tiana as his wings propelled them at super speed through the water and the little girl laughed. It seemed she would be expected to hitch a ride for any travel, and she couldn't deny that it was definitely fun to travel that way.

She soon learned that the usual method of travel,

unless they were in a hurry, was with Amitiel holding Tiana's hand and pulling her along. She pulled them deeper and deeper until the dark started making Tiana more than a little nervous. Amitiel looked at her confused, not sure why Tiana would have problems with the dark. Tiana got the question but wasn't sure how to answer, and not just because of her unfamiliarity with the language.

Amitiel studied the strange human for a moment as she considered her next move. Would this be another situation where it would be best to force the issue, or should she ease the chosen into this a little more slowly. She could read the apprehension coming from the little girl and finally decided that this was one of those situations where she should be patient. The waves had warned her that she would have a lot of those. She pulled Tiana back up to where there was enough light to see by, if only barely. Perhaps when she was more accustomed to the feel of the water she wouldn't feel so encumbered by such a limited thing as vision. Unfortunately, it would limit their diet as well.

Fugl didn't have the problem of a limited diet. There were plenty of large sea animals at this depth, though Tiana did nearly worry herself sick during his tussle with a huge shark that was almost the same size as him. Fugl managed to win the fight though without being more than a little banged up. His biggest setback had been the fact that he wasn't used to his food fighting back and it caught him by surprise. After that, he tended to stick to dolphins and whales for the most part preferring not to work so hard for his meals, but there was more than once that a shark was his only option.

Amitiel had gradually brought them deeper and deeper, and by the time the light was completely gone, Tiana barely noticed anymore. She could feel the comfort of the water surrounding her. In its vibrations she could almost see everything. From the tiniest fish to the largest whale, it was almost like the water was singing to her and she could see why Amitiel seemed to love it here. That didn't mean there was nothing to see though. There were often little light shows. Amitiel's body in particular, gave off a slight glow at this depth, but there were many different types of fish and other sea life that did so as well. Even some of Fugl's spots turned out to be luminescent under the water.

The deeper water also brought new delights to the dragon's diet, though the giant squid were even more trouble than the sharks. The fact that they tasted so much better made it worth it to the picky dragon though who never failed to give chase to a squid. He also took a great liking to eels, which made up a good portion of Amitiel's and Tiana's diet as well, along with kelp and algae. It wasn't long after they'd reached the darkest depths that Amitiel began leading Tiana back to the surface.

Staryn and Mina had quickly picked out a good cave and pulled their cart, still serving as the satyr's bed, inside. Staryn had picked this cave for one main reason. The ancient tree standing in the corner of the entrance. It would make things much easier when the storms came. Speaking of the storms, Staryn began to gather things he could store so that he would have to go out less in the worst of it. Berries didn't stay good for very long off the vine, so he would have to go out at least once a week for them. Nuts, leaves, and barks however, would keep for the full storm season. After questioning Mina on the best things for her to eat during that time, they took the cart out and loaded it with bundles of grass and even a few branches that she identified as appealing.

Over the next two weeks before the storms started, that was how they spent their afternoons. Mornings were spent with Mina exploring and grazing, and Staryn in deep study with the trees. Once the storms hit, he would spend nearly every moment in such a position, but needing time off to gather supplies for the coming storm was nothing that they weren't used to. They knew that Staryn was not nearly as durable as they were and even they could take damage during the worst of it.

Mina tried to wait out the storms in the cave with Staryn. She really did. She got very restless though. She was no stranger to being out in the storms, having never had a shelter to run to before. If Staryn was able to pay more attention to her, it may have been different, but he was spending nearly every waking moment in what seemed to her like silent conference with the trees. The only time he ever paid attention to her was meals, and for an hour or two after dinner before they would fall asleep and she was bored. So much so that she started heading out to explore even with the storms. She always made sure to return by the evening meal, though. It made Staryn a little less jumpy.

Both had noticed that with Tiana gone, Staryn felt the need to be a caregiver to her instead and it irritated her greatly, but she attempted to keep the peace, often reminding herself that it was here or being all alone with no one to talk to. Not to mention she had made a promise to Tiana. She would be very glad when Tiana was back as a buffer though. She understood where it was coming from. Staryn was essentially created to be a caregiver. It was in his nature. In the nature of all satyrs since the beginning of time really, but it was even more so for him, given his unique situation. She couldn't deny that it was nice, in a way, that Staryn worried so much about her, but it got very old very fast. Even though they were born on the same day, relatively speaking, she was far older than him, well into adulthood, while he would remain an adolescent for at least twenty more years, satyrs having longer lives than most other beings, including humans. Needless to say, she found it frustrating to be babied by someone who was practically a baby himself.

By the time the storms were tapering off, they were both more than ready to get out of that cave and despite it still raining, they headed back to the beach. They were both determined to be there the moment Tiana arrived, even if that meant waiting a few days for her to arrive. It ended up being a full day since the rainfall completely ceased and Linaria's suns began to shine once more before Staryn noticed the top of a dark head of hair approaching the shore. "Mina!" he called out to the unicorn he was down the beach some ways. "She's coming!"

He didn't even need to hear the hoofbeats to know that she was winding her way back to him, post haste, and he didn't take his eyes off the water even as Tiana came closer to the shore and once she reached the water shallow enough for her to walk he ran forward, ignoring the itchy feel of the salt water on his fur and met her halfway picking her up and swinging her out of the water with tears of joy as they both clung to each other as tightly as they could. They stood there for a long moment, waves breaking around them, as they just reveled in the feeling of being together again. The moment was broken by Fugl though, who bumped his nose against Staryn in greeting, not quite realizing his own strength anymore between not having the water to soften the blow and the fact that he'd nearly doubled in size during the two months they'd been down there. As a result, both Tiana and Staryn landed in the water and the satyr came up sputtering as Tiana laughed.

They made their way back towards the shore so that Tiana could greet Mina and the reunion was nearly as emotional as it had been with Staryn. Even Fugl and Mina were happy to see each other, which was a near miracle given that they had never gotten along particularly well. "How long do you get to visit?" Staryn asked even as he scratched the now giant dragon on top of his head.

"Two weeks, Amitiel said. Then I have to go back until after the next storm season," Tiana told him.

"Better than I expected but less than I hoped. I guess we'll just have to make the best of it, won't we?" Staryn said with a grin before jumping forward and grabbing Tiana in another swinging hug. "Come on. I'll show you where we've been staying. We'll stop for some food along the way," Staryn told her. "And you can tell me all about life in the water."

Tiana grinned and followed Staryn chattering away a mile a minute, but had to call him to slow down after a moment. "Give me a little while to get used to walking again," she admonished with a chuckle before picking up her litany again, telling him about every little thing she'd seen. Every fish, every piece of seaweed, every meal she'd had. She explained the water language as much as she could and how she could 'see' with her whole body. They all got a good laugh out of the dragon's adventures with ill-tempered food.

It was after dark by the time they got back to the cave and none of them could stay awake much longer. Fugl seemed to have missed Staryn nearly as much as Tiana had though as when they laid down to sleep, Staryn was the one in the middle instead of Tiana as was usual. When he thought about it, it did rather make sense. The dragon had always seen Staryn as a sort of secondary parent after Tiana and he had been gone for two months. It wouldn't be surprising for him to be a bit clingy during this visit. Staryn wouldn't mind a bit though, he thought as he wrapped one arm tightly around Tiana and the other rested on Fugl's head. He'd missed being wanted; being needed, even. For the first time in months, he got a good night's sleep.

Much like Tiana had to get used to walking again, Fugl had to get used to flying again and he brought the rest of the group a great deal of amusement as he kept crashing into the ground when he forgot and tried to use his wings like flippers. The forest had given Staryn a 'vacation' while Tiana was visiting, so this time was just for them to re-forge their bonds as a group and have fun, and have fun they did. Mina mostly played tour guide, having explored much of this area during the time that Tiana had been gone and the mountain made a wonderful playground for a little girl, her guide, and her dragon. Mina didn't 'play' as much as she just watched the others with enjoyment, of course, being far too refined for such indignities.

When the time came for Tiana to return to the sea, it was both less and more emotional than last time. This time, Tiana wasn't afraid or apprehensive. She was leaving one friend to go to another. Leaving one place she loved to go somewhere else she also loved. It was harder too though, since she'd had so little time with Staryn and Mina, and now she was leaving for even longer than she had last time. Only the fact that she knew she would see them again gave her the strength to stand there on the beach and say goodbye. She could see Amitiel's head bobbing out in the water waiting for her, and she wasn't surprised that she wasn't coming to shore again. She had learned how uncomfortable that was for her last time.

She waved at Amitiel to let her know she'd seen her and then turned to Staryn and jumped in his arms. Only the fact that he had been expecting it allowed him to catch her without stumbling. "I'll miss you, kiddo," Staryn said, choking up a bit, despite trying to stay strong for her.

"I'll miss you too, Staryn," she said, not even trying to hide her tears as she wept shamelessly on his shoulder. "You'll be here when I come back again?" she asked imploringly.

"Always, little Tia," he vowed, pressing a kiss to the top of her head before nudging her down to say her goodbyes to Mina and he turned to Fugl. "I'll miss you too," he told the dragon, scratching his head. "You two keep taking care of each other yeah?" Fugl nodded and rubbed his oversized head over Staryn's chest affectionately causing the satyr to stumble backwards a few steps laughing. Tiana came back over and climbed up on Fugl's back, holding Staryn's hand until they had moved too far away into the water when she gave a big wave before they dove beneath the surface. It was a very depressed satyr and unicorn that headed back to the cave.

Chapter 16: The Village

What Tiana had failed to realize just yet was that for every bit of magic she put into the world, the world gave back as the age-old cycle began to ramp up. As her magic leeched out into the world, there were new beings born every day. The waves birthed new mermaids, the trees birthed new satyrs, unicorns, dryads, elves, all of them were returning to the world, slowly but surely. Tiana's studies under the sea were teaching her to use her powers in new and exciting ways, as a matter of course. Instinct, rather than reaction. Her magic was no longer to serve a purpose. It was a part of her, and the world was responding.

Her two years under the sea was long and grueling, but also fun and exciting. Among other things, she became fluent in the language of water, 'seeing' through it, shaping it, creating it, and so much more. It answered to her without question, as did the creatures of the sea. They were her friends, her confidants, her people. Even those without the ability for complex thought. No, *especially* those. Her swim speed was much faster now, able to match Amitiel in a race since she was able to use her powers over the water to propel her in the absence of fins, and many of their last days were spent racing around the deepest oceans. Neither of them could match Fugl's speed though. He was practically a blur racing through the water.

As wonderful and amazing as it was, her visits to the surface with Staryn and Mina were a breath of fresh air, both literally and figuratively. She missed them dearly every moment she was away and looked forward to being able to be with them again. If only it wouldn't mean leaving Amitiel behind when she did. No matter where she went, she would always be leaving someone behind, and thus one of the hardest lessons of life was learned by the now six-year-old girl. Even if she'd had a choice though, it would be Staryn. He would always be her choice. That didn't make it any easier to leave Amitiel though and their parting was filled with nearly as many tears as her initial parting with Staryn was. At least all water, unless contained, was connected. Every lake, river, stream, pond, brook and puddle, and they could all be used to contact Amitiel at any time.

She had learned all she had come to learn, yet Amitiel informed her that the water would send her another teacher soon. One that would teach her more practical uses in the dry world. For now though, they were simply enjoying spending the last bit of time together as they waited for the current storm season to pass when she would return to Staryn and Mina for good. When the time came, Amitiel came with her most of the way to the shore, though she didn't want to leave the water again, so she left Tiana and Fugl to travel the rest of the way alone after a long embrace with them both.

Tiana walked out of the water and rushed straight

into Staryn's arms, and much like every time she had come back for a visit, he picked her up and swung her around, holding her just as tightly as she held him. Once she had said a nearly as exuberant hello to Mina as well Staryn grabbed her arms and held her in front of him. "Look at you, Tia. You've gotten so big," he said cheerfully before pulling you into another hug. "I can't believe how much you've grown up the last two years."

"You're one to talk," Tiana teased as she ran a hand over his remaining horn. "You finally have your curly horn." Neither of them ever spoke of the incident that had lost him his other horn, so they just pretended it was perfectly normal.

Staryn laughed. "I guess I do."

"So, what now, oh wise guide?" Tiana asked playfully.

"Now, we take a day or two to relax. We have a lot to catch up on," he told her with a grin. "Then I have a lot more to teach you about the forest."

"As long as we can do it while we're moving. I think I've had enough of this area," Mina chimed in. The restlessness she had experienced during the first separation had only gotten worse over the years. She had often travelled farther and been gone for as much as weeks at a time, only returning when her need for company overwhelmed her desire to roam.

"Sure thing. Why don't we cross the river and head that way?" Staryn suggested. They decided to leave the cart behind, none of them wanting to trudge back to the cave to get it. It's only purpose really had been as a bed since Staryn had recovered, and it wasn't really worth it to trudge it around anymore, and Mina had admitted that she felt closer to them when they rode on her back instead of behind her, so it was an easy decision.

First though, Tiana wanted to find another village. After two years in the sea, her dresses were rather threadbare, not to mention she could barely squeeze into them anymore as much as she'd grown. The hem was far too high, and the sleeves barely reached her elbows. Besides which, after all that time eating nothing but seaweed and fish, she would kill for some milk and bread. Staryn wasn't a huge fan of the idea, but unlike last time he didn't shoot it down and instead worked with her on ways to make it as safe as possible. None of them had any idea that word had spread from the last village about the kind little witch who left beautiful baubles in return for food and clothing.

It was three days to the next village though, so Staryn decided that he would begin to teach her after their stop and those days were spent catching up on everything they had missed during the two years they had been separated and Tiana showing off a bit of her new powers. Now that she was able to create water, there was no need to keep the water jar full, though it was easier to drink from, and during the times when they were far from any bodies of water, Tiana would use her vines to create a trough for Mina to drink from since she was unable to use the jar. '

Staryn and Tiana had taken to riding Mina during

the afternoons again as Fugl flew overhead. He still wasn't nearly steady enough in the air for either of them to feel comfortable riding on him yet, though Tiana in particular was rather anxious to do so once he adjusted to the difference between swimming and flying. They had both warned him to stay just above the treetops and not get too close to any villages in the air. He was a little too big now to navigate through the forest easily, but when they stopped for the night they always made sure there was a large enough space for him to land and move around.

Tiana's shelters grew much larger as she and Staryn had taken to curling up together on Fugl's back to sleep, though Mina still preferred to sleep in the open, only letting Tiana make a shelter over her head when it rained. She didn't mind the rain per se, but it made the little girl feel better if she slept out of the rain. When they reached the village, much as they had last time, Staryn and Mina waited in the trees with Fugl perched on the nearby mountain, his excellent eyesight allowing him to keep an eye on things without being close enough for the villagers to see anything more than a blurry shape. He took great care to be still so that he could be mistaken for a boulder should any attention be sent his way. Like the others, he took the protection of Tiana very seriously.

While in many ways, it was a good thing that Tiana had been so at peace for so long and was now more comfortable with herself, there were some ways that it was a bad thing. Being less fearful also made her less careful. She found what she was looking for in the fifth yard she slipped into, but as she was pulling two of the dresses off the line, a voice called behind her, "What are you doing?" Tiana jumped in fear, dropping the dresses and turning to run, but the voice called again, "Wait, little one." Perhaps it was something in the tone of the voice, or perhaps it was the appellation that she had long associated with loving care, but she stopped and turned warily to face the stranger, still ready to run, but willing to give her a chance. That was when the woman noticed the beautiful doll in her hand. "You were going to trade that for the clothes?" she asked gently. Tiana nodded slowly. "May I see it?" she asked holding out her hand with a warm smile.

Tiana shuffled forward enough to put it in her hand before skittering back again. "It's very beautiful," the woman told her. "I think my daughter would love it. My name is Caoimhe. What's yours?"

"T-Tiana," she said nervously.

"That's a beautiful name, Tiana," she said with a smile. "I think this doll is worth more than a few old dresses that my daughter is nearly grown out of. How about you come in for supper too?" she offered. Tiana turned to look back towards the trees where she knew Staryn and Mina were watching, probably rather nervously, biting her lip as she considered. It had been so many years since she had a real cooked meal, but was it worth the risk? "You have friends out there?" Caoimhe asked.

"N-No! No, I don't," she said quickly. Too quickly.

"Well I was going to say if you did, they would be welcome to come in for supper as well," the kind woman said gently. Tiana was on the verge of running again. She knew too much. What if she sent someone after Staryn and Mina? Caoimhe saw her thoughts reflected in her face and sought to put her at ease. "There are stories you know, of a child with great powers who roams the woods and gives gifts in return for food and clothing. They say that she travels with those who are not quite human. I've long hoped that she and her companions would come here and that I could offer her something in return for her goodwill. You haven't happened to see her out there, have you?" Caoimhe asked, avoiding the words witch and demon, given their negative connotation. She couldn't imagine how this little child had been treated in the past to be so skittish now.

Tiana narrowed her eyes studiously at the woman, looking deep into her light brown orbs. Reading emotions wasn't nearly as easy as it was through the language of the water, but some of it did carry over, with some effort. She could read that some of the woman's motivation was to gain the goodwill of someone who could do good for her, but mostly she just wanted to take care of her. It was much like the feeling that she had always gotten from Staryn, but with an undertone that was more what she imagined a mother might be like. Perhaps if she had Staryn with her and Mina nearby she would be safe. She still had her mental connection with Fugl and could call him for help if she needed it. "My friends...they can look a little frightening. One of them...people have called him demon, but he's not. He's a satyr. A child of the trees. Of life. But people are scared of him," she warned the woman.

"And I would imagine they are frightened of you too aren't they, child?" she asked sympathetically, and Tiana nodded. "Well I have never met a satyr, but I can promise that he, and you, will be safe here. Will you come in?"

Tiana looked back towards the trees again, taking a moment to make up her mind before waving Staryn and Mina forward and then looking to where she knew Fugl was watching and motioning him to stay. If Tiana didn't know any better, she would have suspected Staryn and Mina of teleporting over since before she knew it she was pressed behind the satyr with Mina in a defensive position in front of them both. Caoimhe raised her hands in a peaceful gesture. "I will not harm any of you. You have my word," she told them and both newcomers relaxed a fraction.

"What's going on, kiddo?" Staryn asked evenly, not taking his wary eyes off the woman.

"She caught me looking for clothes and offered for us to join her for dinner," Tiana told him placing a calming hand on his back.

"You think she can be trusted?" Staryn asked with slight incredulity. "She's human."

"You will find, young satyr, that we people who live near the sea are far more open-minded than many you may meet. Nothing is so unpredictable as the sea and it often seems to have a life of its own. That which kills can also save, and we recognize that far easier than most. If you come in peace, I will treat with you in peace."

Staryn could feel the truth in her words, and relaxed more, placing a hand on Mina's back as well in a calming gesture. "The we will treat with you in peace as well," he said with a nod and Mina moved to their side. "I am Staryn, and this is Mina."

"Pleased to meet you Staryn," she said with a nod before turning to Mina as if trying to decide how to treat her. Talking to a horse would be ridiculous, but she was obviously more than a horse. She just wasn't sure how much more.

"She is intelligent, but for some reason those without magic are unable to hear her words," Staryn told her.

"Then it is wonderful to meet you as well, Mina. I must admit, I am unsure of what someone like you might eat." She didn't want to assume that she would eat the same as horses after all, but Tiana confirmed that she did so Caoimhe went and got some of her horse feed and a bucket to give the unicorn. "And what might you eat, Staryn?" she asked warmly.

"Nuts and berries mostly," he told her.

"And pie. He likes berry pie," Tiana chimed in ducking the hand that swatted playfully at her as Caoimhe laughed.

"Pie I can do. I had just set one out to cool. My

daughter will return from her lessons soon. Would you like to come inside?" she asked.

Tiana looked to Staryn who gave a tentative nod. "I will wait out here," Mina offered, intending to keep watch and listen to make sure nothing went wrong. She could almost trust this human, but had no such trust for any others that might happen by.

Staryn took Tiana's hand, as much for his comfort as hers and followed Caoimhe inside looking around with bright eyed curiosity. "This is a human home?" he asked.

"Yeah. It's a little different than the one I lived in with my father, but mostly the same," she told him.

"Where is your father now, Tiana?" the kindly woman asked, and suddenly wished she hadn't when she saw the sad look cross Tiana's face. Tiana just said that he died, but wouldn't elaborate on how and she didn't have the heart to keep questioning. It was none of her business anyway. "I'm sorry, little one," she said sympathetically. "You're welcome to stay here, if you like," she offered.

"I can't. I still have a lot to learn about my powers and stuff I need to do," Tiana told her. "Thank you though," she added as an afterthought.

"Here. Why don't you change into this and you can take it with you. It will probably fit much better than the one you are wearing," she offered handing her one of the dresses she had been trying to take.

"Thank you," Tiana said gratefully, heading into the next room that Caoimhe had indicated.

Caoimhe could see how nervous Staryn was at being away from her. He got very jittery and didn't take his eyes off the door she had disappeared into, so she tried to draw him into conversation. "Do you mind if I ask...why do you only have one horn?" She could tell by how it was placed at the side of his head instead of the center that it probably wasn't intended that way.

"There was an accident a few years ago. Some people were chasing us and trying to kill us, and my horn got caught and broke off and I was hurt really bad. I nearly died. Tiana and Mina saved my life," he told her.

"You have all been treated roughly by people in the past, I see. I hope that you realize we are not all so cruel," she prodded.

"I do now," he said honestly as Tiana emerged from the room in her pretty new dress.

A few more questions and Caoimhe got the story of what magic used to be before it was corrupted and what Tiana hoped to make it again. "A big job for such a little girl," Caoimhe said sadly. "I wish you all the best on your journey, and hope you are able to find kindness in future villages you pass through on your travels."

About that time Caoimhe's daughter, Esti returned home and, as expected, fell in love with the doll that Tiana had made her. "May I do some magic?" Tiana asked nervously, wanting to give them a little something more for their kindness and Caoimhe nodded while Esti looked on excitedly wanting to see it. Tiana raised her hand and twitched her fingers causing vines to weave and shape into a beautiful little cradle that was a perfect fit for the doll, but would also be a good fit for a living baby as well. Esti gleefully put the doll in the cradle and hugged Tiana tightly in thanks.

Caoimhe, seeing that they would be fine, went to the kitchen to start on supper. Tiana greatly enjoyed playing with another little girl her age and Staryn watched on fondly, glad that she seemed so happy, but not dropping his guard completely. Caoimhe called them in for dinner and placed a bowl of stew in front of the two human girls and a salad in front of Staryn. "The green stuff in it is called lettuce. I wasn't sure if you'd ever tried it before, but since you like nuts and berries I thought you might like it. If not, you can feel free to pick it out," she told him.

Staryn tried it tentatively before a smile broke out on his face and he nodded. "It's very good. Thank you."

She smiled brightly at him before pouring out some milk for the girls. "Would you like some milk too, Staryn?"

"No, thank you. I don't drink milk. Water would be wonderful, though," he told her she nodded and got a large cup of water to set in front of him, watching in surprise as Tiana stuck her finger in it first and then looked in the glass to see that the murky well water was now crystal clear.

"That's handy," she said, shocked.

"I can clean your well water before I go too," she offered, fully intending to fill it if needed as well.

"I would greatly appreciate that," Caoimhe told

her. "But only if it's not too much trouble." She didn't want her to have to work too hard, after all.

"It's not trouble at all. Water and life are my specialties," she told her.

"Then thank you," Caoimhe said with a grateful nod. "Why don't you stay the night and tomorrow you can clean the well and I will go get you some food from in the village to take on your journey."

Tiana looked at Staryn who shrugged. If she wanted to stay for one night, he wouldn't stop her, even if he wouldn't likely get much sleep. Tiana accepted the offer and spent some time after dinner weaving some baskets for Caoimhe to trade for food and a couple for her to keep or trade for herself as well.

"You have a wonderful talent," Caoimhe told her as she inspected the baskets. "These are beautiful. Worth far more than anything we can give you." Craftsmanship like this would take a master crafter nearly a week for each basket and as such they were very rare and very expensive.

"Your kindness is worth far more," Staryn told her seeing that Tiana was too overcome to speak as he reached over and pulled the emotional girl to his side comfortingly. He had meant every word. He could see Tiana's faith in humanity being renewed by being here, as was his own, and that could only bode well for the future. After all, how could she return magic to the world of men if she feared them so much.

Tiana and Staryn, unwilling to separate for the night, shared Caoimhe's bed that she insisted they take.

After all, who knew when or if they would see another bed again. The next morning, she headed into town, leaving Esti with them at both girl's insistence and with Staryn's offer to watch over them until she got back. She couldn't deny that he had done a wonderful job of taking care of Tiana for so long, so she accepted. While she was gone, Esti showed them the well and helped to lower Tiana into it while giggling so Tiana could clean the water. This soon after the storm season, it didn't need to be refilled though, so Tiana walked through their garden, brushing her hands against all of the plants, sending her power into them to grow big and strong.

They spent the remainder of the morning playing with Mina, who Esti fell in love with, and even stayed for lunch before they left. Caoimhe hugged both Tiana and Staryn tightly, surprising the satyr more than the girl and told them, "Be safe out there, and I hope to see you again someday."

Chapter 17: Storms

Once they were back on the road, they circled around the edge of the village and Fugl met back up with them nearly pouncing on them to make sure they were okay. Staryn knew that they should stop soon so that he could start teaching Tiana the forest magic, but he wanted to get some distance between them and the village first. He couldn't deny that Caoimhe and Esti were nice, but there was no telling how the rest of the villagers would react once word spread, and he wanted to keep them ahead of any potential hunters. It was four days before he felt they had gone far enough and they settled in for the more hands on lessons. He had been talking to her about it while they were travelling but now they would stay put for a while and put things into practice.

Tiana's first lesson was in how to hear the trees. She found that their language was something of a cross between spoken language and the water language. It was based somewhat on emotion, but not quite as light. It had more of a steady and strong feel to it, and it was accompanied by impressions more than words. Staryn told her that with practice she would be able to translate those feelings and impressions into words to be able to understand their meaning as clearly as he did. Along with learning to understand them, she was also learning to sense them. Not just their minds, but their physical aspects as well. She learned how to tell where the veins of sap were, allowing her to find where it was closest to the surface and thus easiest to get to for healing. She was learning how to feel their connection to their leaves and how to tell when the connection was weakening enough for them to be removed without distress.

They stayed in the same area for two months as she learned these things, spending many hours of every day sitting and listening and feeling. Staryn was right there with her, guiding her and explaining, bridging the gap between her and the trees and teaching her to narrow it. Tiana realized in those times just how much like the trees he was. While they were all connected, she could feel that his mind carried the same flavor, though it had a great many similarities with hers as well. It truly was a hybrid between trees and humans, but she could sense a wilder undercurrent to it as well and she wondered if that was his connection to the beasts of the wood, which he confirmed when she asked. Another way he was like the trees was his steadfast nurturing nature. It didn't take long at all for her to get the same comforting feeling from them that she always had from Staryn.

After two months, they were all starting to get restless again, so they started moving. They spent nearly a week walking, during which time Staryn told her about her next lessons and the things she would need to know going forward. She still wasn't the best with the language and sensing, but she was far enough along to move forward. She would get better over time. Once they stopped again, Staryn quickly noticed an opportunity for a teaching moment, even if it wouldn't be the most pleasant. He had her put her hand on the tree and reach out with her senses and she jerked back with a cry of pain. "W-what's that?" she asked with a shaky voice looking at the tree with sympathy.

"The last storm broke one of his branches, but it didn't come all the way off so now it's just hanging there," Staryn told her.

"What can I do?" she asked.

"Why don't you ask him?" Staryn suggested with an encouraging smile. Tiana nodded and put her hand against the tree and tried to read what he was telling her. She could feel Staryn with her, probably making sure she didn't misinterpret anything and after a moment she pulled away.

"He said it would be best to just remove it rather than try to heal it right?" she asked to confirm.

"Yep. That's right," Staryn told her proudly. "That means there isn't enough still connected to bother with healing. So let me try to walk you through how to use your powers to finish breaking it off."

"But won't that hurt even more?" she asked worriedly.

"For a minute, yeah. But then it'll be better after that and it can start to heal."

It took a few days before Tiana was confident enough in her ability to do so, and she felt bad for making the tree wait that long, but it had been very understanding about it. He said that he had lived with it for weeks now, a little longer wouldn't hurt anything, and thanked her for even trying. Granted, she could have just climbed up there and pulled it off, but between the fact that she wasn't exactly comfortable climbing up that high and the fact that it would do more damage, she decided against it.

This ended up being her first of many lessons on how to use her powers to affect the trees without hurting them. Once they finished that section a few months later, they moved along again, walking for another week for the lecture part of the lesson before stopping for the hands-on part, this time learning to listen to and affect the animals. They didn't have an actual language like trees did, but they did have feelings that could be read. She learned how to tell if they were scared or hurt or hungry or cold or any of a dozen other things before learning how to use her powers to help them. It helped that they were naturally drawn to her and, as long as Fugl wasn't around, happily came to her when she asked.

Unlike the trees, the animals couldn't understand her speech though, so she had to project impressions and feelings, much like a more rudimentary version of the tree's language, to communicate with them. It also helped her hone her very haphazard and heavy-handed healing skills, and Mina was a good part of those lessons, since she was the natural healer, and Staryn gladly let her take the lead, only jumping in when Mina started explaining things using big words and getting impatient that Tiana was having trouble understanding her. He could tell that she was trying, but she had a tendency to forget that Tiana was just about to turn seven years old, so he acted as translator when needed.

About this time the weather started getting colder as well, especially at night. That was the reason that Staryn had turned their trip north towards the desert regions when Tiana came back from the sea. She wasn't really able to be affected by the cold down there due to the nature of her connection with the water, but she was definitely able to be affected up here. Staryn and Mina had their own protections against the cold with Mina growing a thicker undercoat and Staryn's fur doing the same while the upper part of his body began to harden into something not unlike bark covering his skin. Tiana had no such protections though and Fugl quickly picked up on that causing them to spend some time each evening collecting firewood for Fugl to light. His body heat as they slept on him helped as well. When they were stationary, they made sure to keep the fire going even during the day when needed, but when they were moving, there was no need or ability to do so. They did ride less and walk more during those times though to keep from getting too cold.

A few weeks after they had stopped here it was time to start preparing for the storm season. Fugl had already been scouting for a while and shifted them to the east a few days ago towards the large mountain in the distance, telling them that there were caves there they could hole up in during the worst of it. It had taken about a month of being back on the surface before he was able to communicate with words rather than the language of the water that he had gotten so used to during his formative years, but now he was able to communicate easily with them, though he wasn't exactly talkative most of the time. His boisterous exuberance wasn't exactly suited for long conversation. It was more hyper bursts of things like 'Hey, guess what I found' or 'Watch what I can do'.

It was three days before they reached the base of the mountain and found a problem. It was far too steep for them to get up. Fugl had a solution though. He crouched down and told Staryn and Tiana to climb on his back and hopped up in the air, wrapping his forearms around Mina's middle and flew them up, all three of them screaming, though for different reasons. Tiana was screaming with glee, loving the ride; Staryn with terror, not being a big fan of heights; and Mina with rage at the dragon's impudence of picking her up and flying her like this and wanting nothing more than to just get her feet back on the ground.

When they landed at the entrance of the cave, Staryn slid bonelessly off the dragon, and just barely stopped himself from kissing the ground in relief. Mina stabbed Fugl with her horn, but Tiana just hopped off with an exclamation of, "That was great! Thanks Fugl!" They quickly found that this mountain, while steep at the bottom, wasn't nearly so steep at this height. There was a narrow ledge outside the cave that dropped off sharply, but to the sides there was a much more gradual incline. The ledge was thankfully large enough for even Mina to walk comfortably, though no larger than that and Staryn did get a little woozy if he looked down, but they would deal with it. It was much colder up here though, but as a contrast, there was much more available firewood as the trees shed their minor branches as well as most of their leaves.

There were still a few berry bushes bearing fruit and they quickly cleaned them off, storing them up for the storms before starting on the nuts. By the time the first cracks of lightning lit the sky and the downpour started, they had a good little nest, helped along by the bear that Fugl had killed in order to secure this cave for them and roasted little bits at a time for Tiana. He had no problems hunting in the storm so this one was for her. Since Tiana had plenty of meat, she left most of the nuts and berries for Staryn and she had no interest in Mina's branches and grass.

For the first two weeks of the storms they were able to keep up their lessons outside before it got too bad. When the storms lasted for six weeks at a time, it was necessary to work through them to some degree. The middle two weeks though, not even Mina left the cave. Fugl was the only one crazy enough to go out in it. They even had quite the menagerie of animals hunkered down with them. Mostly the smaller ones and only after Mina promised them that no one would eat them. Fugl mostly preferred larger game, though when two deer wandered in, she had to lay down the law with him. They came to her for protection and they were going to get it. Fugl could do his hunting elsewhere.

Once the worst of the storms had passed, the animals began to trickle out, back to their lives, but the group of friends stayed put for a while. Staryn started taking Tiana back outside to work with the trees and the ground some more, using the opportunity of the saturation of the rain to teach her more about the connection between life and water. Her knowledge of the water combined with her newfound abilities with the trees easily allowed her to follow the path of the water that nourished them, and she understood now why elements of their languages were similar with as deeply as they were connected.

The trees on the mountainside had a different outlook on things than the trees on the flatland. They had different experiences and different dangers. The biggest difference for them though, was that due to the sheer cliff at the base of the mountain, they had never known humans. They had legends of satyrs from their forebears, but had never known an intelligent being before the small group had descended on them. As a result, they stayed much longer than they usually did. The lessons they were learning here couldn't be learned elsewhere, not to mention the fact that they had a lot to teach the trees as well.

Neither Tiana nor Staryn had realized just how much the interaction with humans had affected the forests they had travelled through. Even those who were deep enough not to have any personal contact were affected by others that had and that influence had spread. This, here, was what the forest would have been had humanity never touched this world. Tiana struggled with the language a little more here, the trees speaking in what could only be described as a thicker accent without the little touches from humanity that brought them closer to her way of thinking. When she started to get discouraged though, Staryn lifted her spirits by explaining that it might be more difficult right now, but it would help her greatly in the long run.

Staryn was learning a lot himself, as well. There were legends and stories that had never passed to the forests he'd known. They lived differently as well. Their branches were thinner, even in the summer months, they stored more water for the leaner times between storms, and Staryn and Tiana learned that it was because the water tended to continue downhill at a faster rate and there was less soaked into the ground, which also increased their connection with water due to the storing process. The biggest difference though was the depth of their roots. The trees told them that it was to better hold on to the side of the mountain in the face of the storms, but it also made them less likely to move around. They were far more sedentary and slow to change.

Mina was far more restless than Staryn and Tiana since they were so enamored with their learning so, much like she had when Tiana was in the sea, began to disappear for longer trips, exploring further and further out from where they were. Tiana felt bad, like she was neglecting one of her first friends, but both she and

Staryn assured her that she was doing exactly what she needed to do. Learn. Mina's wanderlust was just as easily sated alone. As long as she had someone to return to in order to stave off the loneliness, she would be fine.

Tiana was also learning a great deal about the animals that she had never seen before that lived on the mountain as their lessons moved further upwards. She was surprised that none of them had come to their cave, but the trees informed her that they all had their own caves that they sought refuge in for the storms. After her long talks with the trees she learned about the different ways to adapt to the different environment and was able to spot those differences; the thicker fur, the cleft hooves, the bodies more streamlined for balance rather than speed. Most of all, she enjoyed getting to know the different animals.

After many months, when the next storm season was about to approach, they started working their way back down the hill, collecting food as they went. By the time the storms were starting, neither of them had seen Mina for two weeks and they were starting to get worried. She had been gone for longer, but the storms made it a different story. Much of that first week of storms was spent worrying until she finally stepped into the cave, shaking herself dry. "Where have you been?" Tiana asked worriedly.

"I didn't realize how far I'd gone. It's no matter though. The storms aren't very bad yet. We still have time before they get too dangerous," Mina told her.

"You don't know that!" Tiana protested. "You never know what can happen out there in the storm. Even when it doesn't seem so bad." Staryn looked taken aback at how vociferously she'd said that. This was only their second storm season together due to her time under the sea, but now that he looked back on it, she had been rather eager to find somewhere to wait it out, and didn't like to go far from the cave when they were outside in it. "Are you afraid of the storms?" he asked concerned as he reached out a hand to her shoulder comfortingly.

"No!" she denied quickly. Too quickly.

"Come on, little Tia," Staryn urged gently. "Talk to me."

"The storms weren't supposed to be bad yet when the sign fell in the village either," Tiana finally said shakily and Staryn understood. She had managed to hide her trepidation last time because they were all together and safe, but this time, with Mina missing, it had brought up all those horrible memories from the incident that cost her home and her father. The storm wasn't supposed to be bad but something bad had happened and people had died, and she had been blamed. It was no wonder the storms made her nervous.

Staryn pulled her tight against him. "It's okay, kiddo. We're all here and we're all safe. Mina will make sure not to be gone when the storms start again, right?" he said aiming that last word at the contrite unicorn who took that opportunity to walk over and nuzzle against the traumatized little girl.

"I'm sorry, child. I did not realize that my absence would cause you such distress. I will ensure that I always return before the storms start in the future," she promised.

"It's okay to cry, Tia," Staryn told her softly when he realized that she was trying to hold it back and that was enough to open the floodgates as she let all the fear and worry and guilt go, sobbing herself to sleep in Staryn's lap.

Chapter 18: Corann

The next morning, Mina decided to explain why she had been so late returning. "So, there was a reason that I was so distracted from the time," she told them now that everyone was calm.

"What happened?" Staryn asked concerned, suddenly all business.

"I met someone," she told him.

"What kind of someone?" Tiana interrupted with wide-eyes.

"He said his name was Corann, he lives in a lake just over a week away with his family. He said he was something called a Kelpie, whatever that is."

"A water sprite," Tiana told her, remembering from Jaren's stories and some brief mentions in her book. She remembered what they looked like from the visions she had received in the grove and could only imagine Mina's confusion at meeting him. He would look quite different from anyone else they had met thus far. "That's where I'm supposed to go next."

"Are you sure?" Staryn asked. He had been planning to head a different direction.

"Amitiel told me that the water would be sending me another teacher. Mina had to have found him for a reason. I'm sure. That's where we go next."

Staryn shrugged. "You're the boss." She was learning to trust her instincts more and that was only a good thing now that they were on their own and had no more clues to follow. He had known to take her to the grove that had sent her to Neri who had sent her to Amitiel, but now they were flying blind save for Tiana's gut, and it was his job to trust that.

The remainder of the storm season was spent with Tiana grilling Mina for the little bit she knew about Corann and telling both Mina and Staryn the little bit she knew about kelpies in general, Staryn occasionally chiming in with some lesser known fact passed down by legends from the forest. Tiana's excitement at meeting a new friend was contagious, and none of them could wait to get back to their travels.

Tiana insisted on waiting until the storms had completely stopped before they set out, which put them leaving a week later than the rest had wanted, but after hearing about why the storms bothered her, none of them could bring themselves to argue with her. Travel was a bit slower with the whole group given Tiana's young age, so it took them nearly two weeks to reach the lake that Mina had found only to find a rather impatient kelpie standing at the side of it. "You're late," he said gruffly.

"I-I'm sorry," Tiana stammered as Staryn just gave the kelpie a hard look that he ignored.

"When I sent the unicorn for you I expected you weeks ago," he told her.

"We had to wait for the storms to pass before we came," Tiana tried to explain.

"Excuses," he brushed her off. "When I'm done with you, you won't have to worry about the storms anymore. Come. We're already behind," he told her as he turned to head back into the water on his spindly frog like legs.

Tiana blinked at him for a moment before she started following the tiny kelpie that barely reached her waist marveling at the way that his green skin turned almost brown once it was underwater. Staryn and Mina stayed back, knowing that they would be more of a hindrance than a help when it came to water, but Fugl started to follow her before Corann turned back. "Only the chosen. No distractions," he told Fugl who whimpered sadly as he sat back on his haunches to mope.

"How long will she be gone?" Staryn asked apprehensively, remember the last time he'd had to say goodbye to her at the water's edge.

"She will return at nightfall to sleep and we will begin again at sunup each day," Corann told him curtly. "Now come."

Tiana looked fearfully back at Staryn even as she followed the curt creature into the depths, and Staryn gave her the most reassuring smile he could manage given the circumstances, hiding his own trepidation at Corann's attitude as much as possible. He wouldn't rest easy until she was back though.

Tiana followed silently to the bottom of the shallow lake where she caught sight of dozens of much smaller kelpies scattering out of sight before her full attention was on the blast of water that was sent at her by Corann that sent her spinning. It hurt a little bit, but not badly. It was more the surprise of it that had her bursting into tears. "Enough sniveling, child. You have learned the peace and comfort of water and now it's time for you to learn its strength. You have a great many trials ahead of you, that you will fall to unless you toughen up."

His words pulled a very different emotion from Tiana who straightened herself up and plastered a look of determination on her face as she snapped, "Why don't you try teaching instead of attacking then?"

Corann let out a loud laugh. "That's more like it," he said with a hard grin. "And as far as teaching, that's what I'm doing. You must first learn to react, to defend. You have all the building blocks you need, or you should if the mermaid did her job. This is something you can only learn by doing, so do it," he said as he sent another blast her way. Tiana threw her arms up in a panic, surprised when this time it barely moved her backwards at all and she kept her bearings. "An adequate first attempt. Now control it." he said with a nod drawing back to blast her again.

The remainder of the day was spent in the same manner, with Corann sending blasts of water at her and her gaining a little more control over it with each try and she was exhausted when he finally released her for the day. Staryn was waiting for her at the water's edge and picked her up when he realized she could barely stand. "What did you do to her?" he asked Corann accusingly.

"I'm giving her the tools she needs to survive. She

will become more accustomed over time," he said coldly before turning to head back into the water.

Staryn managed to rouse her enough to eat some berries before letting her sleep. He could see that her magic was depleted, but not dangerously so. He just hoped that Corann would go easier on her tomorrow. He worried that those hopes would be dashed when the next morning, no sooner than the suns had begun to rise in the sky, webbed feet wandered into their camp, shaking Tiana awake and unintentionally waking Staryn with her. "Can't you just let her sleep?" he asked indignantly even as Tiana started to stir.

"No," Corann said simply as she sat up and started rubbing her eyes. "Come. You are late. Again."

Staryn sighed with frustration and pressed a handful of berries into Tiana's hand as she was sleepily dragged towards the water and she absentmindedly popped them in her mouth, not fully waking until she was submerged. "Your magic is weak," he accused. "We will need to remedy that. In the meantime, today, you will not block. You will simply dodge." He was nice enough to wait for her to nod before he began his relentless assault. He could have easily hurt her badly, but he kept the blasts weak enough to sting, but not do any real damage as she tried and mostly failed to contort her body away from them for the entire morning. She had a great deal of practice with swimming, but spinning, ducking, rolling, and such things were somewhat beyond her still.

By the end of the day, she was managing to dodge

about half of the blasts, but Corann quickly burst her bubble by telling her that he was barely trying. It was a disheartened and once more exhausted child that pulled herself from the lake that evening, gratefully collapsing in Staryn's arms and letting him feed her some berries before she was too deeply asleep to chew anymore. The rest of the week continued similarly and Staryn was growing more and more concerned. At least the kelpie was watching her magic levels and from what few words he'd managed to get out of Tiana, was only having her use it for half the day.

After that first week though, he started breathing easier as she seemed to handle it better. Whether it was because she was getting used to it or because he wasn't working her as hard, he wasn't sure, but she was at least mostly awake when she returned in the evenings and he could sense her magic getting stronger already. Whatever he was doing was working, but he could tell that Tiana was still emotionally fragile. He had learned better by this point to try and gain any sympathy from the kelpie so it was on him and Mina and Fugl to cheer her up, which was made easier by the fact that she was a little more awake these days.

Staryn took every opportunity to tell her how proud he was of her and how strong her magic was getting. He even started singing her something that she called a lullaby that she had often sung over the years. Fugl took every opportunity to wrap her up protectively and rub his giant head against hers and even the usually distant Mina got in on the action, echoing Staryn's

217

praise. By the time the first month had passed, Tiana's spirits rising as well as her magic, the affection from her friends...no, her *family*...doing wonders.

After the second month, they were all surprised to see the water flow out of the lake and form a large opaque blue dome around the lake and surrounding area. Tiana's eyes got wide as she took it in from inside the dome and turned just in time to duck an ice lance from the smirking kelpie. "You have learned to move in water. Now let's see you move on land," he said as he began pulling water from the lake and tossing ice lances at her as she ducked and dodged and rolled, finding it much easier to do so without the water slowing her down and she was amazed at her reflexes. It wasn't until that moment that she realized that maybe the kelpie knew what he was doing after all.

The suns were high in the sky when he barked out, "Now block," without pausing in his assault and a wall of vines quickly popped out of the ground to shatter the sharp ice that was thrown at her. "No. With water," he snapped, and she faltered a bit. It was one thing to use the water that was surrounding her to absorb or deflect more coming at her, but she didn't know where to begin on this one, so she kept dodging as she tried to think. She learned that Corann had been telling the truth in that he was barely trying as the more she dodged the faster and harder he threw until one of the icicles tore a gash in her arm. He did stop at that, but had little sympathy. "I said, *block*," he snapped harshly as she put a hand over the gash on her arm and healed it.

"I don't know how," she snapped back.

"Then figure it out. Do *not* dodge again," he told her taking a stance and giving her a second to prepare before he started again, at his beginning speed. Tiana didn't realize the fact that the ice was softer now until it hit her and just barely managed to take the wind out of her. The next three shots hit her too, until her frustration had her throwing up her arms and a wall of swirling water appeared in front of her. She was so surprised by it, that she didn't even notice the ice bouncing off the dome and coming at her side until it too hit her.

She had an idea at that point and shrunk the wall into a shield, just big enough to cover most of her torso and allow her to peek over the top, and she managed to catch Corann's proud grin as he picked up the speed and the first one she felt shatter against the shield, she knew was back to it's previous near deadly strength. Over the course of the next month, they worked like this with Corann bouncing the ice off different points of the dome to attack her from all sides until she was spinning like mad throwing the shield around and managing to block about ninety percent of them and dodging the ones she couldn't block.

After the third month, Corann pulled Staryn into the dome with them and Tiana looked at the kelpie fearfully. "A leader's job is also to protect her people," he told her before turning to look at Staryn. "You do not move."

"Tiana?" Staryn asked her nervously, willing to trust her judgement more than the kelpie's.

"You will not hurt him," Tiana told Corann in a dangerous tone.

"That is up to you, child," Corann told her and Tiana squared her shoulders and nodded at Staryn who then got a good show as he got to see some of what Tiana had learned over the last few months and he was nearly in awe. How had the kelpie managed to turn such a delicate little girl into a force like this in just three months?

Corann let Tiana dance around the satyr for a few hours before he grew a wave of ice from the ground to rock them apart as he kept firing. Corann knew that the next lance would hit Staryn so he intentionally softened it, but Tiana didn't realize that so when she saw it hit she screamed a denial and called her own ice lance to throw back at the kelpie who easily dodged it. "Now we're getting somewhere," he said with a challenging grin as the ice flew fast and hard between them, him calling his own water shield to deflect what he couldn't dodge. He was still skilled enough to keep up with her fight, keep her blocked from getting to Staryn who was now pulling himself to his feet, and throw a few blasts at Staryn as well, suppressing his grin when her shield flew from her arm to block them while she dodged until it returned to her. He had suspected that the guide was the key to pushing her limits, and it seemed that he was right. Her attacks were sloppy and slow, but they would get better with practice. He would make sure of it.

At the end of the day he dropped the dome and Tiana breathed a sigh of relief as she rushed over to Staryn. "Are you okay?" she asked worriedly looking at the light bruise on his sternum from the hit he took.

"I wouldn't say no to a little healing, but I'm good," he told her. "You were amazing, though! I would never have believed it if I hadn't seen it with my own eyes. How did you learn to do all that?!"

Tiana just blushed and shrugged. She didn't even know how to explain her training to him, so she just let it go, keeping up her blush up until she fell asleep less than an hour later as Staryn regaled Mina and Fugl with stories about how incredible she was long into the night. The rest of the month until the next storm season hit was spent refining her offensive abilities and when the storms started, she finally saw what he meant by not having to worry about the storms anymore. He raised a dome again, but it was different than the one they used for training. It allowed the rain through as the water dripped steadily around it, but had just enough cohesion to deflect all but the smallest debris that was being flung around. Staryn had needed a bit of healing when he learned the hard way not to touch the translucent dome when it got struck by lightning, but otherwise they were perfectly safe.

While the storm was raging the entire group was inside the dome so they all got to see her training, and they had to admit that Staryn hadn't been exaggerating at all. The fact that Corann had more available targets was offset by the fact that he couldn't bounce things off the dome, though Tiana did have to stop Fugl from eating the kelpie more than once after he got hit with a bolt of ice. Fugl was the one that got hit most often, simply because Tiana knew that his thick skin could take the blow better than Staryn or Mina and Corann seemed to enjoy putting her in a position to have to choose. Fugl understood, and made sure she knew that he didn't hold it against her, but it didn't make him any less irritated to be hit.

After the storms were over, the others were locked out again as the kelpie began to teach her close combat skills for the remainder of their time together which lasted another six months until the end of the next storm season, when he announced. "I have given you all the tools you need. It is up to you to use them. You have done better than I expected," he said with a slight bow, which she returned with a smile. "Should you have need of me, you need but call. We all serve the chosen."

"Thank you, Corann. For everything," she told him unable to resist the urge to pull the squirming and protesting kelpie into a tight hug.

"Now begone, child. Until we meet again," he said as he fled...err retreated...err walked very quickly back into the water before she could hug him again.

Chapter 19: Isi

Tiana had no idea where to go next, but when Staryn asked her she just followed her instincts like he told her to do and picked a direction. They had been walking for more than a week before they had a visitor. They had just sat down for the evening meal when there was a flash of flame beside her that soon faded into a red and gold bird that she recognized. "Neri!" she cried happily. "You're back! Are you feeling better than the last time I saw you?"

"I am. I have been reborn and spent a few years travelling. I see you have been learning much. Your power has grown greatly," Neri told her appreciatively. "As have you."

The now almost nine-year-old girl grinned at him. "Why are you here? Will you be teaching me too, or did you just come to visit?"

"A little of both," he told her. He had come to check on her progress and see if it was proceeding apace. He realized that she was quite a bit ahead of what he expected. He would have to step up his other work a notch to keep up. "I am a being of fire and air, neither of which you have much ability with, but there are ways to maximize the little ability you have. I will only be teaching you of air though. Someone else will teach you fire, and I will teach your large friend too," he told her motioning to Fugl. The dragon's power was much more limited than hers overall, but when it came to the elements she had minimal talent with, they were a good match, so would learn at the same rate. He would need to take care to hold them back though, lest he get even further behind.

He managed to drag it out until the start of the next storm season, but he had taught both Tiana and Fugl to hear the whispers on the wind, see magic to a rather limited degree, and call a soft breeze which was all Tiana could manage, though Fugl could manage quite a bit more in that area, pulling a wind strong enough to knock them all off their feet. He left them again just two weeks before the storms began and Fugl asked her if she wanted to call a dome or find a cave.

"If there is a cave nearby we can do that and just use the dome when we need to go out for something. No point wasting the power if we don't need to," she decided, so Fugl went out scouting. By the time he returned, he had found a perfect cave that he assured Mina was at ground level as Tiana groaned jokingly. Fugl would take her up for a ride anytime, and often did, just for fun, so she wasn't too upset about not needing a lift to the cave, but she found Mina's reaction to the idea funny.

As the storms began, their cave once again became a refuge for the smaller creatures in the area pretty early on. About halfway through the second week the first herd of deer came in along with a surprise. Another magical being. Her lower body was that of a deer but where the neck and head would be was the upper body of a little girl about Tiana's age and Tiana quickly pulled her aside, recognizing her from the book and Jaren's stories as a dryad. "Hi. I'm Tiana. What's your name?" she asked her.

"I call myself Isi," she told her with a soft lyrical voice, brushing her long brown hair behind her ear revealing a trail of dark spots across the top of her forehead and down the back of her face and the sides of her neck. "I've never met anyone else that could talk other than the one who taught me," she said amazed.

"Who taught you?" Staryn asked curiously. He had been taught by the trees in preparation for his role as Tiana's guide, but it was a difficult process and only possible because of his deep connection with them and their ability to reach his mind directly.

"He said his name was Neri. He was a bird," Isi told them.

"Neri! So that's where he was," Tiana said excitedly. "When did you see him? How was he?" she asked wondering how long it had taken him to really recover from his incarceration.

"He seemed fine, but I don't know much about birds to know for sure. He didn't say anything was wrong. He didn't stay with me long. He said he had lots of other people to see too. He just told me that I would need to know how to speak for when I met the chosen, whatever that means."

"Tiana is the chosen," Mina chimed in. "The magical child who will unite us all."

Tiana shrugged sheepishly with a bright blush as the dryad turned to look at her in awe. "I'm just a kid like you. I'm still figuring all this out myself," she protested. She didn't think she would ever be comfortable with being put on that kind of a pedestal. "Is that your family you came in with?" she asked curiously, trying to change the subject.

"They are my herdmates. We were all born the same spring, though they are getting close to old age, and I am still but a fawn," she said with the air of one who was long used to being confused by the matter.

"I think you age the same as me," Tiana told her. "I'm pretty sure we were born at the same time and you look about my age."

"You age slowly too?" Isi asked glad to have an explanation at last for something that had puzzled her for her entire life.

"Well, I age normally for a human and since you seem to be half human, you must have gotten your aging from that half," Tiana said with a shrug. It was the most likely explanation. "Would you like to travel with us once the storms are over?" she asked hopefully. It would be nice to have another friend. Isi looked wistfully over at the remainder of her herd, so Tiana said, "They would be welcome too if they want."

"I don't know. They aren't really the type for adventures. We've lived our whole lives in this area," she said.

"But you want an adventure," Mina guessed. She knew Isi's situation well. Her herd had also been content to roam the same place, but she had wanted more. Isi nodded, so Mina said, "Then come with us. It will be fun, and we'll take good care of you."

Isi looked to Staryn for his thoughts. She quickly pegged him as the leader of sorts and she wasn't going to accept without his blessing. "We would love to have you," he said warmly.

"Perhaps I will. I will think about it," she promised. Fugl's return that evening after his hunt found him quite confused at the newcomer. Tiana had made it clear that all within the cave were not suitable for eating, but they still smelled like food. This one though smelled like both food and friend and he wasn't quite sure what to think of her. It took a few days for them both to get over their trepidation about each other enough to sit down and talk it out.

Over the next few weeks, Isi and Tiana became best friends. Tiana finally had someone her own age around and she was enjoying it greatly. The other animals that had taken refuge with them wandered back to their lives once the worst of the storms passed after two weeks, including the rest of Isi's herd. The entire group spent the evenings together and Isi quickly claimed a sleeping spot at Fugl's side, tucking her legs beneath her as she lay down. As the storms were ending, Fugl had come to Tiana and told her of the being he had found in a crater at the top of the mountain and Tiana knew that was where they had to head next, so they started climbing.

It was a long, hard road to the top of the mountain, and Isi in particular wasn't handling it well. Between Staryn and Tiana they managed to keep her motivated and moving though. It didn't help that this mountain was pretty much barren rock, unlike the last and the heat seemed to be radiating up from the ground as well as coming down from above. It took them two long weeks to get to the top, and Fugl started leading them around one of the sides, circling around many small craters where the rock seemed to be cracked and red-hot magma bubbled up from the fissures. None of them had ever seen anything like it, but the heat radiating from it was enough of a warning not to get too close.

Tiana had been so distracted by her surroundings that it took her far longer than it should have for her to notice the huge living flame that they were approaching, and her steps faltered. She didn't think she had ever seen a more intimidating being in her life and for someone who had a dragon the size of five houses as a companion that was saying something. This thing wasn't nearly as big as Fugl of course, only standing about twice Tiana's height, but dark red-orange flames that it was made from as well as the armor of molten rock around his center and head, made for a very imposing sight as she whimpered and hid behind Staryn. Only the satyr's own pride kept him from seeking cover as well. Isi wasn't quite as prideful as Staryn or as determined as Tiana though and she quickly made her escape, followed by an, "I should go after her...make sure she's okay," from Mina who left just as quickly.

Fugl seemed surprised at their reaction and Staryn stopped short when he saw the fire being's approximation of shoulders slump in a universal gesture of sadness and he just blinked at the sight for a moment before gathering his courage and squaring his shoulders to take the lead here. "Hi. I'm Staryn," he said with as much confidence as he could muster.

"Afoz," the rumbling growl coming from the being said.

Staryn could feel Tiana gathering herself behind him and he reached back and gave her hand a comforting squeeze as she stepped out said, "I'm Tiana."

"You are the chosen," Afoz rumbled.

"Yes, and I think I'm supposed to learn from you if you'd be willing," she said shakily.

"Anything for the chosen," he said with a low bow.

"Thank you," she breathed out a sigh of relief.

"What would you like to learn?" he asked.

"Well I'm guessing you're supposed to teach me about fire," she said with a shrug. "I don't think I'll be very good at it though. Neri said it's not a talent but I should still be able to do some."

"Then come learn, chosen. Your companions are welcome to stay with you as well," he offered.

"Thank you," Staryn told him. "I don't know if Mina and Isi are coming back though."

"I saw that they were frightened of me," he said sadly. "I wouldn't hurt them."

"Well you do look kinda scary," Tiana said bluntly. "But you seem nice."

"I do try. I've been so alone up here for so long. I

can't go far from my pools and no one ever comes up here. Not even the trees or the birds," he said, and Tiana got the impression from his voice that if he were capable of it he would be crying and only the fact that he was made of fire kept her from going over to give him a hug.

"I wish I could help you," she said just as sadly. "But I can stay for a while so you can teach me, and if I can I'll come back to visit sometimes," she promised.

"You would come visit me?" he asked heart wrenchingly hopeful.

"If I can. I'm on a bit of a quest and I'm not sure how busy I will be, but I'll do my best." Tiana used her connection with Fugl to send him a request and he turned to look at her in shock.

"You want me to stay? You don't want me with you anymore?" he asked.

"Of course, I want you with me Fugl. You're one of my best friends. But this really would be the best place for you. You have so much trouble getting through the forests now and Afoz could really use the company. Plus, you fly really fast, so you can always come see me often even when we're far apart and I can still call you if I need you. It doesn't have to be goodbye. I don't *want* it to be goodbye."

"I'll think about it. I'll decide before you leave," Fugl promised and the hope he could see in Afoz' stance nearly had him saying yes right away. Fugle had never been alone before. He had always had Tiana. He had accompanied her everywhere. He couldn't imagine how sad it would be to be alone all the time and he definitely didn't want to leave someone else like that if he could help it. Could he really leave Tiana though? At least he had time to decide.

They spent the rest of the day just chatting and getting to know the sensitive fire elemental, marveling at the contrast between his imposing appearance and his gentle demeanor. He even pulled all the heat from an area at the corner of his mountain for Tiana and Staryn to be more comfortable as they slept on Fugl's back, doing his best to take care of any of their needs. Since it was a long walk up and down the barren mountain, Fugl was sent with a sling, not unlike the one that Tiana had carried his egg in for so long, to retrieve nuts and berries for Tiana and Staryn. His fingers weren't nearly as nimble as theirs so most of them were a bit smashed, but he had soon figured out a trick to lay the sling under the bush and shake it.

Fugl had found Mina and Isi at the base of the mountain and tried to convince them to come back up but they both refused, and in fact, told Fugl to tell Tiana and Staryn goodbye for them. Mina knew that they would be up there for months, and the idea of sitting around the base of a mountain for all that time didn't sit well with her. Mina had taken Isi under her wing. They had come from similar backgrounds after all, and she knew that the young dryad was likely feeling rather out of her depth and she was still so young and very much needed a mother. She may have been the same age as Tiana, but the little magician's experiences had made her so much older than she seemed. She and Isi could sate their wanderlust as they tried to find their place in this world, and perhaps gather others like them. There was a bit of an argument over the matter, but in the end Fugl had to let them go.

Tiana didn't cry often anymore, but at learning that one of her oldest friends and her new friend had left them, possibly for good, she couldn't hold it in. Staryn put on a brave face even as his own heart was breaking too, and even Afoz cried tears of hot ash for their pain. For someone who had been so alone for so long, losing even one of your friends was inconceivably tragic to him and he couldn't help but feel responsible. They had left because they were afraid of him. Tiana was quick to reassure him. "It's not your fault Afoz. Really. Mina had been restless for a long time. She doesn't like staying in one place for very long and we stop a lot. The only reason she didn't leave sooner is because she didn't want to be alone either. I guess now that she has Isi she doesn't need us anymore," she said sadly as the tears kept running down her cheeks.

"I don't think it was an easy decision for her," Staryn said sadly, hearing the accusation in her final statement. "You know she was never really happy with us. We were just better than the alternative. It's just like when you told Fugl to stay here because it was better for him. She will be happier out there roaming free with Isi. You wouldn't begrudge her that would you?"

"She could have at least said a real goodbye," Tiana

sniffled.

"And I'm sure she would have if it wouldn't have meant waiting months or longer at the bottom of a mountain for us to come down," Staryn assured her before looking at Afoz. "And that's not your fault either. They both had a difficult time on the climb up and wouldn't want to do it again."

"I know," Tiana said burrowing against Staryn's side as Fugl, being the only one able to get close without burning up, tried to comfort Afoz. "I'm just gonna miss them so much."

"I know, little Tia," Staryn murmured, running a hand through her hair. "Me too."

Chapter 20: Afoz

The next morning Tiana woke up ready to work with a new determination. She had been through enough lessons with the other elements that she just spent the first day asking question after question to try to understand how fire worked. "Does it have its own language? What kinds of beings are of fire? What kinds of things can you do with it?" were among the questions. Afoz had never spoken so much in his life. Even with the chatty fire bird, but he answered all her questions kindly and patiently.

It wasn't until the second day that he started teaching her how to use and understand it, but it didn't take long for Tiana to get discouraged. She had even less talent with fire than she did with air. At least air she could understand at least a little bit, but as Afoz was trying to teach her the fire language, she couldn't even make out anything more than a crackling roar. She couldn't connect to it at all. It was a month before Afoz reluctantly gave up on teaching her to speak with it, and Tiana was very upset until Staryn explained why. "It's not surprising that you have little talent with fire. Fire is about anger and passion. Two things you aren't really built to understand." That made her feel a little better, but it still bugged her. She hated that there was something that she not only couldn't do, but would never be able to do.

"But Afoz isn't angry," she protested.

"Because I have little to be angry about, little chosen," he told her. "I assure you, my anger burns bright when needed." He declined to mention that the last time he was angry the entire mountain erupted. The last thing he wanted was for her to be afraid of him again.

"So, you're saying that fire is dark?" Tiana asked both Staryn and Afoz.

"Anything has the capacity to be dark as well as light," Staryn told her.

"The guide is correct. Righteous anger is light. Uncontrolled rage is dark. Loving passion is light. Obsessive passion is dark. Fire, due to its inherently destructive nature, just skews more towards the dark and so it is difficult for one so completely of the light to control."

"Exactly," Staryn nodded respectfully to the elemental. "Like how you learned to fight with water and with life. Those could easily be turned dark as well, but they are also more tempered. You understand?"

"Yeah. I think I do. So, you think I'll never be able to do anything with fire?" she asked sadly.

"There is still much I can teach you. And perhaps you will be able to do something with it, but we will never know until we try," Afoz told her.

"Perhaps it would be better to teach her defenses against fire?" Staryn suggested.

"Perhaps. I wish to try a few more things to see if she can use it in other ways first though...if you are agreeable, chosen."

"That would be okay," Tiana told him. She really wanted to get at least something figured out. By the end of their third month, she had managed little more than creating a small flame and limited abilities over shaping the flames that were already going. She couldn't stop it or even turn it back, but she could steer it slightly. The fourth month began with Staryn's idea of teaching her to fight the fire with her strengths. Afoz had called up a flame and she had sent a blast of water at it, but some of it splashed the fire elemental and he hissed in pain, pulling his arm back as steam flowed from what could only be considered a wound. "Oh no! I'm so sorry Afoz! Are you okay?" she asked near tears.

It was a few minutes before Afoz managed to speak through his pain. "It is no matter, chosen. Accidents happen. I was as much at fault for being so close to the flame you were intending to douse. We will both be more careful in the future I'd imagine." Tiana nodded ardently, once again wishing she could hug him, but hugged Staryn instead.

"How do you cope with the storms?" Tiana asked, now curious as to what he did when it rained for six weeks at a time.

"I have a small cave within the great crater that I wait them out in," he told her. The few times it had rained since the last storm had been during the night, so she had not noticed his retreat. Linaria seldom had more than light showers between the storms so that made it easier for him. "You are welcome to join me for the next storms if you like, though the heat may be unbearable for those of flesh."

"I have a better idea. Why don't you join us? We stayed in a cave at the bottom of the mountain during the last storms, or would that be too far from your pools?" she asked.

"I believe that would be too far, yes," he said sadly. He could easily go to the bottom of the mountain during the dry seasons, but if he were to go down during the storms he wouldn't be able to come back up for six weeks and he couldn't be away for that long or he would die.

"Well maybe we could find something closer where we would all be comfortable?" Staryn suggested before looking at Fugl who quickly took wing to do some scouting, but sadly was unable to find anything suitable, so it was agreed that Tiana and Staryn would go to their cave at the bottom, which was also near food for them to gather rather than sending Fugl up and down all the time, and the dragon would stay in Afoz cave with him to keep him company. They still had more than a month before the storms would hit though, so they got back to work.

It was only a few weeks later they got a surprise. Tiana was the first to notice that Fugl hadn't moved from his spot for two days, though he seemed just as alert and gregarious as always. "Are you okay? You haven't moved in a while," Tiana asked worriedly. For the constantly hyper dragon, that was definitely a cause for concern. Fugl gave her what she had come to recognize as a grin as he shifted up to his feet for a moment as twin gasps filled the air and Afoz started sparking with excitement. "Eggs!" Tiana exclaimed. "Does that mean you're going to have baby dragons?" she asked enthusiastically.

"Yes. I felt that since I was going to make this my primary residence for a while, it would be a good time to begin repopulating the world with my kin," he told her proudly.

"That's wonderful! But aren't you a boy? How can you have babies?" she asked innocently curious.

"How can trees give birth to satyrs? Or waves to mermaids?" Staryn asked knowingly.

"Magic," Tiana nodded her understanding.

"That is correct, but not in my case," Fugl told them. "Dragons are capable of having babies alone, especially when they are the last of their kind. There are many scaled and water beings that have that ability without magic.

"That's awesome!" Tiana said. "How many do you have? I didn't get a chance to count," she admitted.

"There are five eggs, and since they are born on a mountain of flames they will be born as fire dragons. One day I will birth water dragons and life dragons as well, and my kin will be filling the skies once more," he said wistfully.

Staryn smiled warmly at him. "Fatherhood suits you, Fugl. Congratulations." His well wishes were quickly echoed by Tiana and Afoz who was ecstatic. He knew that Fugl wouldn't be able to stay with him forever, but perhaps one or more of his offspring would make this mountain their home.

Over the course of the last month before the storms, she learned that as well as using water to douse the flames, which she was always very careful with after that first time, she could also use the dirt to smother it. By the time the storm season was approaching, she was very proficient at protecting herself from fire, though neither she nor Afoz were willing to actually have a fight between them due to the dangers, both of her getting burned and him getting wet.

The way down the mountain would be a lot quicker than the way up, and they would be safe if they were caught outside in it anyway thanks to Tiana's command over water and her ability to pull up a shield, so they waited until just a few days before the storms were due to start before bidding Afoz and Fugl a sad farewell. Afoz had reluctantly admitted that he'd taught her as much as he could, so they wouldn't be making the effort to climb back up after the storms. "You'll bring your babies to visit me when they're old enough to travel?" Tiana asked hopefully.

"Of course," Fugl told her as though it should be obvious, as he hugged her tightly against him with his wing which she completely disappeared under. Staryn quickly got the same treatment with the other wing and it was a long time before he let them go as pearly tears trickled down his face. He could feel the moisture against his sides that meant that they were crying too, and even Afoz had tears of ash leaving streaks through the flames that made up his face.

When he finally let them go, they turned to Afoz. "I wish I could hug you too Afoz, but know that I will miss you, and I still remember my promise to come visit as much as I can."

"I wish that as well, chosen, and I will look forward to your visits greatly," the fire elemental sniffled. "And you as well, guide."

Tiana and Staryn were only halfway down the mountain when the downpour started two days later, and it was another four before they reached the cave. They didn't bother drying off at the moment though and instead went out to collect food. Even though Tiana could easily shield them from the storm now, they still preferred to wait out the worst of it inside as much as was practical, so they stocked up well.

It was quite the adjustment being back down to just the two of them, and they were both more prone to fits of melancholy and loneliness, but they leaned on each other, so those times were short-lived. As they considered where to go next, Tiana wanted to find another village, though she was trying to put off that discussion as long as she could, so didn't mention it. It had been a few years and she had grown a lot. At ten years old, she was nearly as tall as Staryn now, him still not looking any older than a human fourteen-year-old would. He had explained the odd aging patterns of Satyrs years earlier. Since the trees couldn't care for an infant they were born the equivalent of a human two-year-old and aged rapidly until they were old enough to require little care. From there, they aged at a greatly decreased rate until they reached full maturity when they stopped aging at all until they reached old age after a few hundred years and their humanoid body died and they were reborn as a tree. Tiana thought it was great that she would catch up to him in the next few years and had every intention of teasing him about being younger than her once she passed him.

This storm season seemed to last longer than the others with only each other for company. They missed Mina's dignified wit, and Fugl's liveliness, but at least they still had each other. Tiana knew that without Staryn she would have no hope to go on, even though she could take care of herself now. He was like a part of her; her other half, and she comforted herself with the fact that his role as her guide was a lifelong one. He would always be at her side, as long as they lived.

As the storms began tapering off, Tiana knew that it was time to talk about where they were going next. "I was thinking when we leave here we could find a village," she suggested.

"I don't know if that's the best idea," Staryn said with a wince. "We don't have Mina anymore for a fast getaway or Fugl for protection," he pointed out.

"You really think I can't take care of myself?" Tiana asked, hurt.

"It's not that. It's just...I don't want you to have to hurt anyone because I know that would hurt you even more."

"I don't have to hurt anyone to get away if something happens. I can trap them in a dome and run," she pointed out.

"And what if they are too spread out and surrounding you," Staryn asked, as much to help her make a plan as to argue against going. He realized that it would be futile.

"Then I can call an groundquake to knock them off their feet, or shield myself in a circle of vines as I run," she told him. The water domes didn't travel with her as well as the vines could unfortunately.

"And how long can you run before you get too tired and they catch you?" Staryn asked.

"I'm sure I could easily outrun them if I needed to, but if not, I can call up vines to trap them and hold them in place until I'm well away. I can do this Staryn. Please let me."

"Okay. As long as you promise to be careful," Staryn told her.

"I will," she promised.

"So, you're just going to sneak in like before?" he asked.

"Actually, I'm old enough now not to be out of place walking around alone so I was thinking I just walk in and do my trading like a normal person and just not draw attention to myself," Tiana told him. "It's much safer that way. It's been six years, surely people have forgotten about me by now, and even if they haven't they wouldn't recognize me anymore anyway. I'd just be another traveler coming through."

Staryn had to admit that she was right. She was more likely to be caught sneaking around than pegged as anything different from just walking around normally. That still didn't make him like it though, but he knew he wouldn't be able to stop her. "Okay, but I'll be watching from the trees like always and if you seem like you're in trouble I'm coming to get you, even if it's just to meet you as you're running. Deal?"

"Deal," she told him with a grin. She didn't think it would come to that, but she knew that if it did, she would feel much better knowing he was there.

When the storms stopped a few days later they asked the trees to point them to the nearest village which happened to be at the edge of the desert region and they set out that way. They soon realized another adjustment they would have to make in that they were much slower without Mina's help. In the end it took them nearly three weeks to reach the edge of the village and they scouted around from their cover for a while before Tiana had a plan of approach. There was a shop right at one edge of the village that held clothes. She would draw far less attention if she were appropriately attired before setting out into the village proper.

She had made a wide variety of things to trade from weaved vines, stone, and even shaped wood that had fallen from the trees. Her best creation though was the small platform with short sides and four wheels, pulled by a vine that she used to carry the things she had to trade. She had a few baskets that Caoimhe had seemed to love, a few dolls, and she made some stuff for boys as well since she would be going to an actual

shop rather than somewhere a little girl lived. She'd
shaped wood into horses, birds, and dogs and had even
weaved her vines into a few hollow lightweight balls.
She had taken a week to get her treasures sorted before
she hugged Staryn goodbye and made her way to the
little shop.

Chapter 21: Barden

Tiana squared her shoulders and put on a mask of confidence, like she belonged here as she stepped in and the woman at the counter gasped at the sight of her. "Oh, my dear! What happened to you?"

Tiana looked down at herself and realized that the woman was reacting to the singes all around her clothing. "I had a little accident with a campfire," she told her. "This was all that was salvageable, so I need some new clothes. I bought some stuff to trade."

"Oh, of course. Come. Let's get you changed into something first and then we can see what you have to trade. Come, child," the woman bustled her over to one of the shelves, eyeballing her for a moment before pulling a dress off the rack that seemed like it would fit her. Even if she had nothing worth trading for she would at least be walking out with the one dress, anyway. No way would she leave such a young girl to wander without anything suitable to wear.

When Tiana came out, she felt much better, and the woman smiled brightly at her. "You look very pretty, child. What is your name?"

"I'm Tiana," she told her.

"Welcome Tiana. I'm Nosipho," she told her. "Now let us see what you have to trade." They went over to the wagon and Nosipho's eyes widened at the selection. "Where did you get all this?" she asked in awe as she picked up one of the carved horses running her hands over it reverently.

"I like making things," Tiana told her with a shy smile.

"You have a great talent, Tiana. These are wonderful," she told her. "How much were you looking to trade for?" she asked, so she would have a baseline to begin their trade.

"At least two dresses, maybe three, and some good walking shoes," Tiana told her.

"Only three dresses? You could get far more than that for what you have here," she told her.

"Well I also need to stock up on food and milk before I go too," Tiana told her.

"Well, let me see," Nosipho said thoughtfully. "How about I take one of these beautiful baskets and this horse and one of these balls for my son. You can pick your three dresses and shoes. You also look like you could use another bag. That one looks rather frayed, and you can come to my house for dinner when you finish your shopping and even stay until tomorrow if you plan to travel. Are you travelling alone?"

"No. I have a friend with me, but he doesn't like coming into the villages when we stop," Tiana told her.

"Well at least you're not travelling alone," Nosipho said. She likely was old enough to be fine, but she still felt better that the girl had a companion. "He is welcome to join us for dinner as well. Our house is just at the edge of the village, so he wouldn't have to be around other people," she offered. She had known many people who chose to live as hermits rather than mix with other people, so she found nothing strange about that.

"He probably won't want to, but I'll go ask him," she lied. "Thank you for your hospitality."

"No thanks needed. My son is about your age and if he were traveling on his own I would hope that someone would show him the same kindness." Tiana smiled warmly at her before going to look at the clothes and picking something out. As she had the last few times, she had gotten dresses that were bigger on her, leaving her more room to grow, and the same with the shoes. She had been using shoes she had shaped from wood the last few years since the ones she got from Caoimhe had become unbearably tight, but these were much more comfortable. When she returned to Nosipho for her acceptance of what she had chosen, the kind shopkeeper presented her with a bag far larger than her old fraying one that she had carried since she was four.

Nosipho told her to meet back here in five hours to come to her house for dinner and Tiana thanked her and headed out in search of somewhere she could eat lunch. Another basket and she had a piping hot meat pie and a large cup of milk placed in front of her and she dug in hungrily. Without Fugl around she hadn't had meat in a while. She had tried. She had even caught a rabbit, but she couldn't bring herself to do it, so she just cuddled her for a while and then let her go. She wasn't even going to consider asking Staryn. He was even more connected to them than she was, so who knew when she would get meat to eat again.

She finished her meal in silence, getting a few looks from other patrons due to her age, but nothing that spelled suspicion or potential trouble. Once she had eaten she headed out to the bread cart first. The man running the bread cart had a daughter and so took one of the dolls and the cradle for her in exchange for four loaves of bread. She went by the meat vendor next and asked for something that would last for a while. He had a variety of cooked meats that would last for a week or longer before going bad, and quite a few types of cured, dried strips of meat that would last for weeks or even months. She took some of the cooked meat and a lot of the dried strips in return for two more of the baskets, leaving her with one of those left.

She had just been planning to get some milk after that, but then she passed a jam and preserves cart and since she still had a great deal left to trade, she decided to splurge a bit. Two of the carved dogs and one of the carved birds got her three jars of different types of jams. A carved horse got her a bag of lettuce for Staryn since he had liked it so much at Caoimhe's and the milk was her last stop. The last basket went for two large jugs of milk and even a chunk of cheese since the man said it was worth more milk than she could drink before it spoiled even with her using her powers to keep it cold.

Her shopping done, she headed back to Nosipho's shop with less than an hour to spare, her cart loaded up with her wares since it was easier for now than carrying them on her back. She had traded everything she had bought save for one of the balls and the cart itself which she fully intended to leave with Nosipho in return for her kindness. When she arrived at the shop, she stopped short at the sight of the boy who was sitting behind the counter. He acted like Nosipho's son, but she knew immediately that he was different. His white windswept hair hung over his light blue-grey eyes, and Tiana could see the magic coiling within him that she couldn't quite place. He wasn't human though, so she knew he wasn't the human boy she had seen born with her. It wasn't until he turned to look at Nosipho that she noticed the points on his ears and she knew. This was the elf child born of the sandstorm.

"Tiana!" Nosipho said cheerfully. "You're back and it looks like you got plenty of supplies. I still have a little time before I close up shop, but you're welcome to look around if you like. This is my son, Barden."

"Hi Barden," Tiana managed to say without stammering before looking back at Nosipho. "I was wondering if I could leave my stuff here for a little bit while I run and see if my friend will come for dinner?" she asked. Once she told Staryn that this boy was the elf, he would surely want to come. They would need to tell him who he was which would likely mean telling his parents as well.

"Of course you can, dear," Nosipho told her, and Tiana gave her a grateful smile and ran out, directly towards the forest where she left Staryn.

"What's wrong?" he asked worriedly, seeing that

she was coming back empty handed, but not being chased.

"A-an elf!" Tiana stammered excitedly. "There is a boy in the village, he's the elf I saw in the grove. He must have been adopted because his mother invited us over for dinner."

"And you think we should go," Staryn said with a sign.

"He needs to know who and what he is, and his parents too," Tiana said firmly.

"Just so we're clear, you realize that will mean revealing what you are too, right," Staryn told her nervously.

"I know, which is why I thought that you could help," Tiana told him, seeing his worry about the situation but not willing to back down on this one.

"Okay. If that's what you think is best, but suggestion?" When Tiana nodded he said, "I think it would be better for you to do the initial explanations, with a good line of sight back to the forest in case you need to run of course, before I come out. Remember people seem to think I'm a demon when they see me."

"Yeah, okay. That's a good idea," Tiana told him. "Nosipho said they live on the edge of the village so you can just follow along in the trees and I'll signal you when you're good to come." Staryn nodded so Tiana headed back to Nosipho's shop before they closed.

"Where's your friend?" Nosipho asked visibly disappointed that she had returned alone.

"He'll come in a little while. Once we're there. He

doesn't want to walk through the village," she told them.

"Good," she said with a smile. "At least he will come."

As she closed up the shop, Barden offered to pull Tiana's cart and she accepted with a happy grin, and they chatted lightly as they walked. "Mother said that you made those things. The horse and the ball."

"I did. I like making things," she told him.

"How did you learn to do that?" he asked curiously.

"My friend taught me," she said.

"What's his name?"

"Staryn. I think you'll like him," Tiana told him.

"What other kinds of things can you make?" Barden asked.

"Lots of stuff. Just about anything with wood or stone or vines. Do you want me to show you later?" she offered.

"That would be awesome!" he said excitedly as they reached their destination.

"Should we go around back and signal your friend?" Nosipho asked already making to do just that.

Tiana nodded and followed her as she considered how to best do this. When they got to the back of the house she knew her time was up, so she squared her shoulders and said, "Okay before I call my friend there's something you should know."

"What is it dear?" she asked.

"He's not exactly human," she told her. "People seem to think he looks a little scary, but I don't know why. He's just a kid like me, but he's a satyr so he has fur on his legs and a horn on his head and people call him a demon, but he's not. He's really nice and he's been taking care of me most of my life."

"I...wh-what's a Satyr?" Nosipho asked worriedly, pulling her son closer to her. "ABU!" she called loudly and a rather burly looking man rushed out of the house just as Tiana started to answer.

"He's a tree spirit. He was born from the trees and his job is to nurture life and care for the forest. Well that's what most satyrs are supposed to do, and he does a lot, but his main job is to take care of me now because I'm magic and I'm supposed to bring good magic back to the world."

Nosipho was now looking at Tiana rather skeptically, and the man openly scoffed. "Magic, huh."

"Please don't be scared," Tiana told them as she held up her hands and called a bunch of vines from the ground and began twitching her fingers forming them into a basket like the ones she had traded without touching them as Nosipho gasped and the man just looked dumbfounded.

"How...what..." Nosipho stammered when she found her voice.

"It's magic. But it's okay. I won't hurt anyone. I just want to help people," Tiana assured them. "There's more too. Barden...he's magic too. I can see it in him."

"No. He's not. He couldn't be. He can't do things like that," Nosipho said worriedly pulling him close.

"He's not quite like me. He's more like Staryn. Not

quite human. He's what is known as an elf. I'm betting he was found alone in the desert when you took him in?"

"How could you possibly know that?" the man said suspiciously as Barden gaped at them.

"It's true? I-I'm not your son?" he asked heart-brokenly.

Tiana suddenly felt horrible as she was forgotten by both parents who rushed to reassure him that it didn't mean that they loved him any less. "I-I'm sorry," she said softly, trying to hold back her tears.

Nosipho was torn between comforting her son and comforting this little slip of a girl. It was a mother's instinct, but she turned her attention back to her son for now. She could worry about Tiana after. They managed to get Barden calmed down though he still seemed a little shaken, and she turned back to Tiana. "So. you're magic, but you don't intend to hurt anyone? You just want to help people?" she asked turning all of her attention on trying to read this girl.

"Yeah, see, back when magic was part of the world, magicians used to have a good relationship with people. They helped their crops grow strong and protected them and healed them, and even made them things they needed, but then they started getting bad and forcing people to be their slaves until a bad war started and all magic died, but now it's back and a lot of us were born at the same time. Me, Barden, Staryn, unicorns, mermaids, kelpies, and lots of others. I went to a place called the pools of knowledge in the eternal grove and saw it all. The past the present and some of the future. I saw Barden being born from a sandstorm in the desert just like I saw the others," Tiana explained.

"Why don't you call your friend over and we can all sit down and talk about this," the man said curtly.

"This is my husband, Abufel," Nosipho introduced him. There was no reason to drop their manners just because they were out of their depth.

"Just so you know, I won't hurt anyone, but I won't allow myself or him to be hurt either," Tiana told them nervously.

"Neither of you will be harmed without cause," Abufel promised.

Tiana nodded and turned to motion Staryn in from the woods and he rushed quickly to your side. "Everything okay, Tia?" he asked worriedly.

"It's fine. Staryn this is Nosipho, her husband Abufel, and Barden. This is Staryn," she handled the introductions.

"You're right. I can see the magic in him. He's a life-giver like you and me, but also of air if I'm not mistaken," Staryn said enamored by the young boy and barely noticing the adults save to ensure they weren't a threat.

"He's really a-an...elf?" Nosipho asked tentatively.

"Yes. He was born of magic," Staryn told them.

"Wouldn't we have noticed before now?" Abufel questioned.

"Maybe not. I was able to hide my magic for a long time and I'm a lot stronger in outward magic than he is.

His is mostly inward. My magic used to show in us having good luck, big healthy harvests, and stuff like that," Tiana told him.

"We really have had things turn around for us in the last ten years," Nosipho said to her husband who seemed to have come to the same realization. "Why don't we go inside, and I'll start dinner while we talk all this out?" she suggested.

All three of the family were rather shaken by the revelations. They had all been under the impression that the only magic in the world resided in their king and his bird. They didn't even know what to begin thinking about this. Tiana offered to help with dinner, making sure that there was something for Staryn to eat as well while Tiana answered questions from the parents.

Staryn, noticing that Barden was still rather out of it, pulled him to the side. "I know this is probably a lot for you to take in," Staryn said sympathetically. Barden just nodded. "I can't say that I know how you feel, but I can say that you're one of the lucky ones. We've met a lot of magical beings in our travels, and most of them have been alone and friendless. None of them had people who loved them or families that cared for them. You have a great thing going here, and your parents don't seem like the type to change that just because they know what you are now."

"The kid is right," Abufel said with a nod to Staryn as he put a hand on his son's shoulder, ignoring the way they had both jumped at his presence. "You're still our son. Elf or not."

Barden looked up at his father and gave him a relieved nod before turning back to Staryn. "You said you've met other magic people?" he asked curiously. "What were they like?"

Staryn began to talk, not noticing that their conversation had drawn the attention of Nosipho and Tiana as well. "Well there was Mina, she is a unicorn and she had been alone most of her life, and was terribly lonely. She travelled with us for a while until we met Isi who is a dryad and shared her wanderlust and they went off to explore together..." Staryn continued describing all of the friends they'd made with frequent commentary from Tiana and the elf and his parents slowly got more comfortable with the idea of magic over the course of the evening before they offered to allow Tiana and Staryn to stay for a while and teach them more.

Chapter 22: Betrayal

Tiana felt the need to stay for a while, even if it meant that Staryn had to stay out of sight of the rest of the villagers. They spent a lot of time in the woods trying to teach Barden over the next few days while Nosipho was in her shop and Abufel worked the fields. Barden usually helped him most of the day, but the man was quick to assure him that this was more important. At least for now. He had no need to worry about the harvest not being good enough anymore after all. Even if he fell behind, he suspected that his son's magic would make up for the deficit.

Tiana and Staryn were having trouble with Barden though. He remained distant and seemed almost afraid of himself, of his magic. He was very resistant to anything they tried to teach him. One day, a few days after they arrived, Tiana was trying to motivate him to speak to the trees, but it was like he wasn't even trying, and she got frustrated, snapping, "Why won't you just cooperate?!" Staryn immediately pulled her back, knowing that wasn't the way, but the damage was already done. Barden had gotten up and ran off, back into the village where Staryn couldn't follow and Tiana wasn't in any mood to do so.

"You have to be gentle, little Tia," Staryn chided gently. "Getting upset will just make him more resistant to learning."

"He's being so stubborn," she huffed.

"Of course, he is. This is all so new to him. You at least knew you had abilities all your life even if you didn't know much about them. He's just now found out that he's magic and on top of that, that his parents aren't really his parents. He just needs some time to adjust," Staryn explained.

Tiana sighed sadly. She knew that Staryn was right. "I'm sorry. I shouldn't have gotten upset at him."

"No. You shouldn't have. He will be back though. If nothing else, we're staying at his house. You'll have your chance to apologize to him," Staryn pointed out.

What neither of them realized was that Barden had enough. He was writing a letter they should have written days ago, when these strangers first showed up. His parents had said not to, but he didn't care anymore. Not when it could mean all their deaths. He would protect his family from their own nurturing natures. These last few days proved that he wasn't what they said. These weren't children like his parents seemed to think. They were magic, and he refused to let them take down his family. He quickly scrawled out what he needed to say and rushed out to get the letter sent to the king as quickly as possible.

None of them had mentioned the king to Tiana and Staryn yet, not wanting to scare them away, but Barden decided it was time. The next day he followed them out to the forest again, and instead of even pretending to try and do what they asked, he told them with a slightly snide tone, "You know you're not the only magic people we've heard of."

"What do you mean? You know of others?" Tiana asked hopefully.

"The king is magic like you," he told Tiana.

"H-he is?!" she asked excitedly, turning to Staryn. "Do you think he's the other magic human baby I saw?"

"It's possible," Staryn said not quite as excited as she was. He wasn't so sure about the idea of a magical human being a king. It was too much authority and it made him nervous, but when he tried to point that out to Tiana once they were alone for the night, she just brushed him off. Her excitement to meet someone else like her was blinding her.

"King doesn't mean bad," she protested. "Kings protect people and help people too."

"But how did he get to be a king?" Staryn asked. "I doubt he was born as one. Have you ever known of another place that had a king? He's obviously not in this village or we would have sensed him, which means he rules over more than one village."

"More people that he can help," Tiana pointed out.

"I don't know about this," Staryn said nervously.

"Don't worry. I'm sure everything will be fine," Tiana told him, steadfastly ignoring that feeling in her gut that was trying to contradict her. She finally knew where the other magical human was and he must be close.

They were woken the next morning by a loud banging on the door. Since Tiana and Staryn were sleeping in the living area, there not being another available bedroom for them, they were the first to get up, but Nosipho and Abufel were rushing down the stairs quickly, and Nosipho motioned for Staryn to hide before she opened the door.

Tiana's eyes widened at the men at the door who were dressed in very formal uniforms, and was confused when both of the adults bowed and Nosipho opened the door wider to allow them in, a hint of fear showing in their faces. "We understand you have found other magical beings. The king is eager to meet them and has extended an invitation for them to join him in the palace," the man with the most ornate of the uniform's said looking at Tiana curiously.

The girl squared her shoulders and stood tall. "We are eager to meet him as well. We accept," she said motioning Staryn to come out of hiding. The only reason the satyr did so was so that Tiana wouldn't end up going alone. There was no chance to talk her out of this now and he only hoped that he could keep her safe if the worst happened. He couldn't help but give her a betrayed look as he stepped out of the closet though, suppressing his smirk when he saw the men falter at his appearance and get visibly nervous before schooling themselves and motioning them out the door.

Tiana grabbed her pack and turned to their hosts. "Thank you for your hospitality. You may keep the cart I made." The fearful and apologetic look that Nosipho sent her as well as the sorrowful one from Abufel made her wonder for the first time if she was making the right decision here, but it was too late to turn back now. She didn't miss Barden's smug look as he peeked around the corner though and there was no more doubt as to how the king had found out about them.

They were led into a black covered carriage, two of the men riding inside with them while the other two took seats up top. The long ride was spent in complete silence, both Tiana's and Staryn's apprehension growing as they looked out the windows. Tiana did dig into her pack and pull out some berries and lettuce for Staryn and some bread and jam for herself for breakfast, and then did the same at lunchtime. By the time dinner had arrived though they no longer had an appetite left after what they were seeing out the window.

There were scores of people dressed in rags lugging boulders larger than they were through the desert and there were a few other men, well dressed, walking around them with whips in their hands. The first time they saw the whip crack over a woman's back, Tiana had to swallow her bile and Staryn closed his eyes to block the images he was seeing. All Tiana could think in that moment was that Staryn had been right and she'd made a huge mistake. She considered using her powers to neutralize the men she now saw as guards and making a run for it, but she couldn't just leave all these people. Not when there was a chance she could help them. Not when she might be able to talk this king down or at least find a way to nullify his power.

After what seemed like forever, the carriage finally stopped in front of an ornate castle that was obviously built on the backs of slave labor. In fact, parts of it were still being built by the people in rags. Tiana stepped out, forcing herself into a mask of calm, not allowing them to see her fear and she could feel Staryn behind her doing the same. He knew what she was going to try to do here. He was just afraid it wouldn't work but he wasn't going to give them the satisfaction of seeing him cower. Especially not if Tiana was putting on a brave face.

They were led into a large throne room and as soon as they entered Tiana's eyes lit on the boy on the throne. He had straight dark hair, nearly black eyes, and his skin was a pale white. He turned his pointed nose up to them and his face lit with a kind of glee that made Tiana feel cold all the way down to her bones. She could feel the cruelty and the hatred rolling off this boy who was the same age as her, but she stood her ground. "So, you are the magic users I was told about," he said with a grin. "I had thought I was the only one. Neri!" he called, and a very familiar bird lit on his shoulder.

"Neri!" Tiana cried in betrayal. "How could you?!"

"Balance, Tiana. As I said before. The darkness and the light," Neri told her from his place on the boy king's shoulder.

"You didn't tell me about them?" the boy asked the bird narrowing his eyes.

"My apologies, King Keevan. They had to find their way to you on their own. My interference would have had disastrous consequences," Neri told him with a slight bow.

"I should have been informed the second they entered my kingdom at least," Keevan snapped before turning back to them. "But it's no matter now. You are here, and you may join me."

"Join you? In this?" Tiana scoffed. "No. We will not join you. You have to stop this. You can't treat people this way!"

"And why not? Humanity will reap what they have sown. They are treated no worse than they treated me before I learned to use my power. Humans fear us. They hate us. We will keep them in line so that they don't destroy us," he sneered.

"They aren't all like that!" Tiana protested. "Most of them are good and kind. The whole reason any of them fear us at all is because of people like you. You think this is teaching them a lesson, but you're wrong. All it's teaching them is that they were right to fear you."

"You can't possibly be so naïve?" Keevan snapped. "Have you ever even been around humans? I would imagine not with your friend being so obviously different. They would have killed him without a moment's thought. And you too for daring to associate with him, even if they didn't know you were magic. You must know that on some level because why else would you avoid them?"

"What makes you think we have?" Tiana asked narrowing her eyes at him trying to keep his words from making sense.

"Because if you hadn't we would have heard about it. Word travels slowly among the villages, but it does travel. There would have been a great deal of talk of one such as him had he ever gone publicly into a village. Why, even in the village we picked you up from, no one outside the family you were staying with even knew he existed."

"That doesn't mean this is the way," Staryn chimed in, seeing that his words were starting to reach Tiana and desperate to stop it. "Tiana is right about people being like this because of people like you. They fear magic because magic has hurt them in the past. Only by showing them kindness can we change their hearts and minds."

"Silence, beast," Keevan said waving his hand and throwing Staryn back to slam against the stone wall.

"Staryn, no!" Tiana cried rushing to his side and immediately putting an ice wall around them while she tried to figure out what to do next as she placed her hands over his head and healed his wound. As he started to wake up, Tiana could feel the strain on her shield and tried to strengthen it, but it was no use. It melted away and she had to duck the stream of fire that followed it. Before she was able to raise another wall, she was struck by a lightning bolt that flew from Keevan's hand and she too flew back into the wall, knocked unconscious more by the electricity of the lightning than the blow to her head, though it hadn't helped matters in the slightest. Staryn tried to get up to help her, to fight, to do something, but his leg buckled under his wait and he couldn't stop the scream of pain as it bent the wrong way. Before he even realized what happened, his hands were tied behind his back and he was thrown over a tall shoulder. He looked up to see Tiana getting the same treatment before he heard Keevan's cold voice say, "Throw them in the dungeons. They will join me, eventually. We will see to that."

Staryn and Tiana were placed in cells side by side, across from a man who was chained to the wall. He looked so frail, like he was barely fed enough to keep him alive and the bruises, cuts, and welts over his body told their own story. He didn't seem to be conscious any more than Tiana was so Staryn sat back to wait. He wanted to try to shake Tiana awake, but when they had thrown her into her cell, it was on the opposite side to Staryn's, so he couldn't reach her. The satyr couldn't say how long it had been before she groaned and stirred awake, but it had felt like weeks locked in this cold dark cell. "Tiana! Wake up, kiddo. Come on," he coaxed.

"Staryn?" she murmured as she struggled to gain her bearings and then the memories rushed back to her and she sat up quickly looking around with wide eyes. "Staryn!"

"I'm right here, little Tia. How are you?" he asked worriedly.

"I'm...okay, I think. A little sore," she said as she checked herself for injuries.

"Good," Staryn said relieved.

"It won't last," a weak voice croaked.

"What do you mean?" Tiana asked worriedly as she took a good look around at her surroundings and choked back a sob at the sight of the man on the wall.

"My son will not leave you in peace for long," he

told them.

"Your...son? Keevan is your son? And he has you locked up down here? He really is a monster!" Tiana said, unable to keep her tears at bay any longer.

"He is what he was made, and I must say that I regret my part in it," the man said sorrowfully.

"Your part?" Staryn asked, not sure if he wanted to know.

"My wife, she died birthing him and he had all these powers. I always knew he killed her and I wasn't going to let him get away with it. But it turned him cold and cruel. He won't even kill me so I can be with her again. He won't save me this pain and torture. He is determined to pay me back ten-fold for every ill I ever put on him."

"You...you hurt your own son?" Tiana asked disgustedly, feeling her sympathy for the man fading.

"You see what he is! He's pure evil!" he tried to defend himself.

"Because you made him that way!" Tiana cried.

"Just forget him for now, Tiana. We need to think of a way to get out of here. Can you call Fugl?" Staryn asked

"Right. Of course," Tiana said relieved as she closed her eyes and tried to focus on her bond to the dragon before they snapped open again. "I-I can't," she said fearfully.

"I was afraid of that," Staryn said defeated. "Neri has taught him well I'm afraid. Too well."

"What do you mean? How could he block me from

Fugl?"

"One of the powers of air is the ability to block any sort of mental abilities, like your connection. You should still be able to use your magic though. That's a part of you that nothing can block. See if you can find a way to get us out of here."

Tiana nodded and raised her hand pulling vines from the ground to wrap around the thick steel bars. They weren't strong enough though. No matter how hard she created the vines, they always snapped before the metal gave way even a little. There was no point in trying anything with water. Even the hardest ice would be futile against the strength of the bars. "I don't think I can," she whimpered.

"Hey, it's okay, little Tia," Staryn said softly as he tried to shift closer to her before letting out a cry of pain as his broken leg dragged over the ground.

"You're hurt!" she said worriedly, her own fear and hopelessness forgotten as she rushed to the bars separating them and reached through, placing a hand on his leg and sending a burst of healing, feeling the bone knitting together beneath her hand. At least this was something she could do.

"Thank you, Tia," Staryn said with relief as he felt the pain fade.

"Don't thank me until I find a way to get us out of here," she said determinedly. She wasn't about to give up yet.

Printed in Great Britain
by Amazon